Praise for

DEL TORO MOON

"...a wildly original, pulse-pounding tale of a boy carrying on his family's legacy of protecting their rural community from bloodthirsty, supernatural skinners. Medieval Spanish myth meets the Hispanic culture of rugged southern Colorado to create a captivating story of modern-day knights."

—Laura Resau, Américas Award-winning author of *What the Moon Saw* and *The Lightning Queen*

"A rip-roaring monster slaying adventure with heart and humor, cleverly situated in the contemporary mountains and canyons of southern Colorado. This fresh and fun exploration of tough familial relationships, modern knights, and talking horses is sure to appeal to fans of *The Ranger's Apprentice* and equine enthusiasts."

—Todd Mitchell, author of *The Last Panther* and *The Traitor King*

THE
RED
CASKET

DARBY KARCHUT

Owl Hollow Press

Owl Hollow Press, LLC, Springville, UT 84663

The Red Casket

Library of Congress Cataloging-in-Publication Data
Red Casket, The/ D. Karchut. — First edition.

Summary: When a menacing witch shows up at the Del Toro ranch and demands the return of the Red Casket, twelve year old Matt Del Toro must team up with his best friend and talking warhorses to out-wit, out-ride, and out-fight a Viking-size sorceress.

Cover Design and Illustration © 2019 by Milorad Savanović

ISBN 978-1-945654-43-5 (paperback)
ISBN 978-1-945654-44-2 (e-book)
Library of Congress Control Number: 2019955946

This book is for Emma,
who opened the corral gate

"First the west and then the world..."

Pest control. That's what our father, Javier Del Toro, jokingly called our hunting sprees. My big brother Ben dubbed those outings the family rodeo. Made sense, since we hunted on horseback—the nearby canyons of southern Colorado that hid our prey were too rugged for vehicles or even ATVs. Me? I simply thought of the excursions as our family's business. The business being creepy critter search-and-destroy. We ran it old-school style, complete with battle-savvy warhorses and magic-powered iron maces.

I had only begun accompanying Dad and Ben a few months ago. The search part wasn't so bad. The destroy part? That was another level of freaky.

As we rode along the dirt road, I eyed our destination. The enormous mesa jutted up out of the prairie a few miles north of our ranch. On the map of Colorado, the mesa was officially labeled *El Laberinto* Wilderness Area. The local residents of the nearby town of Huerfano just called it the

Maze, because of its hundreds of slot canyons, and stayed clear. Even though they wouldn't admit it aloud, most of them believed the centuries-old myth that a wild pack of hairless wolf-like creatures—skinners—with a taste for humans infested the Maze's canyons.

It was no myth.

Shifting in the saddle, I plucked at my T-shirt and fanned it, hoping to dry the sweat already running down my spine, even though the August sun was barely a finger-width above the horizon. Another drought season had bleached the surrounding grassland to a pale yellow. My friend and hunting partner, the bay stallion Rigo, trotted along beneath me, hooves kicking up the dust. Crunching the grit between my teeth, I stood in the stirrups for a few strides.

Rigo peered back, ebony eye half covered by his black forelock. "Stop worrying, Matt. We got this."

"I'm not worried," I lied, wishing I'd skipped that second bowl of cereal at breakfast. With each bounce, it sloshed around. Grimacing, I rubbed my stomach.

"I doubt we'll find any skinners." He shook his mane out of his face. "We did a solid job locking them back inside the coffer."

But that was two months ago, I wanted to say. But bravado, right? Still, I wondered if they found a way to crawl back out.

Next to me, my brother snorted. "Which is why today is a royal waste of time." Mounted on the sorrel mare Isabel, Ben rode slumped and bleary-eyed, like he had just crawled out of bed and into the saddle at the last moment.

Which he had—Ben had a hate-you-no-hate-you-more relationship with mornings.

"Unless we run across some," I said, trying for casual though my palms got sticky-sweaty at the thought of going *mano a mano* with even *one* skinner. I tucked my mace—a club-like weapon with an iron ball on the business end—under an arm and scrubbed my hand along my jeans.

"Then you two noobs can have first dibs," Ben said. "Practice and all that." He poked me with his mace.

I blocked it with mine—a clank of iron on iron. "Hey, I've done my share of hunting. And Rigo has busted more creatures than you and Izzie put together. Haven't you?" I patted his shoulder, then flattened my hand over the rolling muscle. His brown coat was burnished mahogany from my daily grooming.

"You name 'em, I've maimed 'em," Rigo said.

The black stallion trotting on my other side snorted in derision. "Only by luck. I've seen you hunt." Turk's voice was an avalanche's rumble. "You two are barely the JV team."

I made a face at Turk, who sneered back. Like Rigo and Izzie, the black was a classic Andalusian. All three of them had the breed's powerful bodies and legs, curved necks, and sweeping manes and tails that unfurled like banners when they ran. The morning breeze caught Turk's mane, lifting it just enough to flow back over Dad's lap.

Mounted on Turk, our father rode like he had been raised in the saddle. Which he had. Mace in his right hand, he moved in effortless rhythm with the black stallion's jarring gait.

Watching Dad out of the corner of my eye, I copied him, even though I risked being teased by Ben. He knew how much I wanted to be a hunter of all things monster like our father. I knew I never would.

Still…

Heels down, back straight but relaxed. Chin level, and shoulders squared to my mount's. I tried to keep my ankles loose, letting them take the shock of Rigo's trot. Mimicking Dad, I rested my fist and mace's haft on my right thigh, while my left hand held the reins to Rigo's halter. Under me, Rigo arched his neck and picked up his knees just a tad higher. Guess we were both showing off a little.

Dad glanced over. A faint smile pulled his dark goatee to one side. "Behold *el caballero*," he said, saluting me with a dip of his signature black cowboy hat. His amber eyes, a Del Toro trait both Ben and I inherited from him, danced at the exaggeration.

Secretly pleased, I kept my gaze focused on the towering mesa growing closer and closer with each stride. My good mood floated away. I gulped and tightened my fingers around the haft of my mace.

"Hey, Dad?" I tried to keep my voice from doing that squeaky thing. "Do you really think we missed some skinners? We've checked twice already and *nada*."

"I do not. But as we know, the coffer will not hold them in forever." He sighed. "It is too bad, though. As Ben said, we could use the practice."

I didn't say it aloud, but I was just fine *not* confronting one of the wolfish creatures that looked like they were made from rotting hamburger—smelled like it, too—and carried lethal venom in their bite. Yeah, hard pass there.

Too soon for my taste, we reached the southern wall of the Maze. A wide, dark corridor—the Gate—split the towering sandstone and granite wall like a gap in the front teeth of a giant. We paused a few yards from the opening. Cool air flowed from it, chilling my sweat and ruffling the horses' manes. Tilting my head back, I studied the twin buttes on either side of the Gate. The tops of those stony watch towers held magical wards that cast an invisible creature-proof barrier across the opening. The last skinner that had tried to escape the Maze got turned into a patty melt.

"All right, *amigos*." Dad gestured at the Gate. "Do your thing."

Head high and ears pricked, Rigo's nose circled the air, snuffling. "I'm not catching any scent."

"Isabel?" Dad asked.

"Hard to tell, Javier," the sorrel said. Her nostrils fluttered like moths. "Those hairless stinkers could be deep in one of the canyons. We won't know until we go in and do some scouting." She cocked her head. "You guys hear that?"

Ben leaned over and laid a hand on her neck. "Hear what, Izzie?"

"Sounds like an engine. Coming from inside the Maze."

Dad craned his neck. "Turk?"

Turk's ears twitched. "Yeah, a vehicle of some sort. Can't tell what kind."

I stared at the Gate, thinking back to earlier in the summer when a group of paleontologists had set up a camp inside the Maze, thus proving that a person could drive an RV through the corridor if they didn't mind losing a side mirror. That dig had ended in a Jurassic Park–level failure due to the one of the leaders, Dr. Philip Allbury, letting a pack of skinners out of the magical coffer where they had been imprisoned. If it hadn't been for us Del Toros riding to their rescue, those scientists would've all been not-so-happy monster meals.

The engine's whine grew louder, magnified by the tunnel. An older model Jeep, with its top missing, appeared. As it bounced toward us, I noticed the driver, a young man with a sunburned face and a mop of frizzy brown hair, staring at us. His mouth twisted in a mix of fear and frustration. He slowed the Jeep to a crawl, fingers tapping the steering wheel as he inched along.

Shoulder to shoulder, the horses stood their ground like war memorial statues. Only their manes and tails moved, stirred by the breeze.

With the front bumper only a few feet away, the stranger finally clued into the fact that we weren't budging. The Jeep's brakes squealed as he came to a stop. Scowling, he leaned out of the vehicle.

"Do you mind?" He pointed at the road behind us. "You're blocking my way."

"Actually," Dad said, "*this* is blocking your way." At an unseen signal from our father, Turk stomped up to the driver, stuck his nose in the man's face and let loose a mighty snort. The blast blew the man's hair off his forehead.

"What the heck?" Eyes wide, the man huddled back as far as the seat would allow.

"I advise you," Dad said with a smile, "not to move. He bites. Now, before I call him off, I would like to know what you were doing in the Maze."

Eyes still pinned on Turk's nose a few inches from his own, the man gulped. "J-just checking it out. Public land, right? No law against driving in there." His gaze flitted across Dad's faded denim shirt. "What are you—a park ranger or something?"

"A concerned citizen. One who knows there is a law that prohibits the removal of any artifact, vegetation, or wildlife from state or federal land. Matt? Ben?" Our father gestured with his mace. "Check the back."

"Hey, wait a minute. You can't just go through my stuff—"

Turk flattened his ears and let out a low rumble. The guy's mouth closed on the rest of his protest with a snap.

Ben and I swung down. With Rigo and Izzie on our heels, we walked around to the back of the Jeep. Rigo huffed at the exhaust's stink. Wrinkling my own nose, I peered into the cargo area. It was empty, except for a bunched up hoodie and two jugs of water. A corner of a map poked out from under the jacket. I pulled the map free and spread it open, the crisp paper crinkling. Frowning, I held it closer to my face.

It was a topographical map of the Maze. We had one at home just like it, but ours was so marked up with Xs and circles and comments scribbled all over it I could barely read it. This one was new and had only one thing circled in red ink: a spot near the northeast corner of the Maze's central valley.

"Uh-oh." I carried the map over to Dad and handed it up as Turk continued to stare down the man. "Allbury strikes again."

Dad studied it, then re-folded it on the first try and tossed it in the man's lap. Leaning forward, he braced his crossed arms on the saddle horn. "In spite of what Dr. Allbury may have told you, my friend, there are no rare seventeenth century iron chests hidden in a cave—unclaimed and unguarded—in the northeast corner of the Maze," he said, smoothly and blatantly lying through his teeth. "Nor is there a market—black or otherwise—for such finds, even though Allbury swore there was *and* offered to find a buyer if you were able to steal one of the chests. A fifty-fifty split, no?"

The man's jaw sagged.

Dad nodded. "Yes, it is Allbury's modus operandi; you are the second collector he has sent out here. A piece of advice—the Maze is a dangerous place, for many reasons. People have gotten lost, or lost their lives in there. If you value your skin, do not return." He straightened and gathered up the reins. "Turk?"

The black stepped out of the way. For a moment, the man sat there, mouth working. Giving up on the word search, he wrestled the stick shift into gear and stomped on the gas. The Jeep lurched away, tires spinning. Grit stung my face. Rigo snorted in protest and flung up his head.

Spitting to one side, I blinked the dust from my eyes and reached for the stirrup. A sudden realization hit me. My heart rose. "Well, at least we don't have to check out the Maze now."

Rigo swung his head around. "We don't?"

"Nope." I hauled myself into the saddle. "Thanks to that guy, we know there are no skinners loose in the Maze. It's all clear. At least, for now. Right, Dad?"

Eyes narrowed, our father nodded absently, gaze locked on the retreating vehicle.

Already mounted, Ben frowned. "What are you talking about?"

I grinned, secretly proud to be one step ahead of my big brother. "Because if there *had* been any of those creatures in there, they would've attacked the guy."

"Probably *eaten* the guy," Izzie added.

Turk bared his teeth. "And maybe we scared enough bejeebers out of Jeep Guy that word'll get back to Allbury the Maze is closed for business and he better find another way to make a quick buck."

Dad gave the Jeep one last look before it disappeared down the road. "Greed is a sharp spur. There will be others."

"Do you know a Javier Del Toro? Local rancher. Allegedly has a place somewhere around here."

At the sound of a stranger asking about my father, I paused in the middle of the convenience store's aisle. *Aw, man. I bet that's another one.* Sheesh, it had only been a couple of weeks since we'd chased off Jeep Guy. Clutching a package of single serve Pop-Tarts, I crouched down, then crept closer to the shelf and peered between bags of chips.

The clerk, a new employee I hadn't seen before, was talking to a woman. Actually, being talked *at* by a woman. One big-as-Thor woman. Taller than most men, she towered over the counter and over the clerk. Her hair, Nordic white, was cut short and stood up straight from her head in a punk spiky style from the '80s. Dressed like a biker—black leather jacket and faded jeans—her combat boots added another inch to her height.

So, yeah. A biking Viking.

"Sorry." The clerk stared up, trying to act cool and failing. "I moved here like ten days ago. I don't know any of the home brews yet."

I noticed he stood as far back as he could behind the counter without crawling up the cigarette rack behind him. Was the woman holding a gun or a knife? I groaned to myself. Why did I leave my mace in the truck?

Slapping both hands on the counter, the woman leaned closer. "Who *would* know, then?"

"Look, I can't help you, okay?" The clerk's gaze darted around the store. I froze, hoping he didn't remember me coming in a few minutes ago. "Seriously. I'm new around here. Just started this job two days ago. I don't even know—"

"Oh, shut up." The women pushed away from the counter. It wobbled. Packs of Twinkies tumbled to the floor. She stomped on them as she marched past my hiding place and headed for the door, leaving cream-filled footprints in her wake; a piece of wrapper clung to one boot. I caught a glimpse of her face before hunkering lower. Her eyes, a shade of pale blue, were framed by brows and lashes as white as her hair.

Chewing on my lip, I played rabbit and stayed motionless, knees bent and shoulders hunched. My thigh muscles began to complain. I told them to deal with it. The door chime sounded once. A few moments later, an engine—a big motorcycle by its roar—thundered to life. The driver punished the throttle, then drove away. I counted to twenty, waited for the rumble to fade, then straightened with a grimace and shook out my legs.

The store was empty, except for the clerk. Slurping a soda he probably hadn't paid for, he thumbed the screen of a cell phone with his free hand.

Fishing some bills out of my jeans, I headed for the counter. "Who was *that*?"

"Don't know." *Beep.* He scanned my purchase, never looking away from his phone. "Don't care."

Loser. I made a face at the top of his head.

"Yo. Doofus." Ben appeared in the doorway. "What's taking you so long?" He eyed the globs of cake and cream tracked across the floor. "Dude."

"Hey, not mine." I scooped up the change and the package. "Listen. Some woman was just asking about—"

"Whatever. Get in the truck before I leave you here." He stomped away.

Stepping around the mangled Twinkies, I debated mentioning the mess to the clerk. *Not my circus.* I hurried outside.

Even though Huerfano sat near the foothills of the Sangre de Cristo Range, the afternoon's heat smacked me in the face. Jogging across the parking lot's sticky asphalt, my boots made a kissing sound as I checked my six for that woman. I peered around as I opened the passenger door.

"What's your problem?" Ben settled behind the steering wheel. Cranking the engine, he pummeled the gas pedal until it turned over. "You're being all squirrelly."

"Didn't you see that weird woman come out of the store?" I joined him, then fished my mace from under the seat and tucked it between my knees, silently vowing to bring it with me next time. After all, Colorado was an open carry state. "Super tall. Short white hair. Leather jacket. I think she rode a motorcycle."

"No. Why?"

"She asked the clerk about Dad. By *name*. She said she knew he lived on a ranch around here."

"What?" Ben's right hand drifted to his own mace wedged between the seat and console. Frowning, he scanned the area. "Did she know who you were?"

"She never saw me. I hid in the snack aisle. And, luckily, that new clerk doesn't know me. Do you think she's another collector?"

"With our luck?" He huffed out a long breath. "Just what we need. Now Dad'll get all bent out of shape. I'm getting sick of his bad moods."

I didn't say anything. Just yesterday, our father had complained that *he* was tired of Ben's relentless nagging and complaining because Dad wouldn't buy him a car.

Coming together as family earlier in the summer, we had kicked some serious monster tail, rescued a girl—much to her distress because my friend Perry was no damsel—and saved that group of paleontologists which included Perry's mom, Dr. Liz Vandermer.

I had hoped all the near-death encounters would spark some familial love and kindness, but now that the fun was over, Dad and Ben were back at their favorite hobby: fighting with each other. Between the two of them, I was spending a lot of time in the barn with Rigo and Izzie, or hanging with Perry. She was at our house so often that Dad joked about adopting her. I knew Perry wouldn't mind. Neither would Izzie. Those two had become as close as Rigo and me.

"What about Ben?" I had asked Izzie once when Perry wasn't around.

"What about him?" the sorrel had replied. "He's still my partner and *compañero*, if that's what you're asking. No matter what, I'll always have his back. But Perry and I are friends, too." She had nosed my chest. "Like El Cid used to say: we horses have big hearts. They can hold a lot of people."

El Cid.

My eyes stole to the thin woven bracelet tied around Ben's wrist. Braided from a lock of El Cid's white mane, it was a match to the one I wore.

Sorrow fluttered down and settled in my chest like a crow landing on a telephone line. The death of my best friend from a skinner attack was an ache that the last two months had only dulled from punch-in-the-gut grief to foot-dragging acceptance. I wondered if I'd spend the rest of my life with a horse-shaped cavern in my heart.

Ben's cell phone blasted to life with the familiar voice of the singer encouraging his son, who was wayward, to carry on. I knew my brother had only chosen the opening chords because he thought the song irritated the fire out of our father. Dad actually liked it and would sing along when it came on the oldies radio station as long as Ben wasn't around.

"It is one of the few good things to come from Kansas," he would always say afterwards. I never knew if he meant the rock band or the state.

Ben plucked the device from the cup holder and tapped the screen. "Hey."

"I have been thinking," our father's voice rose from the phone, "of renting a larger post office box to sleep in. Since my sons have abandoned me here."

"If you weren't such a tightwad," Ben muttered low enough to escape both detection and retribution, "and get me my own car, this wouldn't be a problem." He didn't actually say "tight*wad*." He said the *other* word that went with "tight" and meant the same thing.

I shook my head. *Give it a rest already*. Leaning over, I spoke into the phone. "We're on our way now." My voice did that funny squeak thing. I ignored my brother's smirk

Ben shifted into drive and rolled out of the parking lot. Two girls in a small car pulled in. One had her bare feet sticking out the passenger window. They honked and waved at Ben, who grinned back. Right then, the truck's engine coughed and almost stalled out.

Swearing under his breath, he goosed the pedal a few times until the engine smoothed out. "I *hate* this stupid truck. And *he* knows it. He's just getting back at me."

"For what?"

"For whatever." Ben scowled.

Choosing not to show up for that circus either, my thoughts circled back to what had gone down in the 7-Eleven. "We need to tell Dad about her."

"No, we don't. You know it fries the *frijoles* out of him when anyone even *mentions* those people. You want him in a bad mood the rest of the day?"

Ben had a point. "Heck, try the rest of the year," I said. Sighing, I adjusted the horsehair bracelet around my wrist. "I wish El Cid was still with us. We could tell *him* about that woman, and *he'd* handle Dad. El Cid was the only one Dad really listened to and—"

"Well, he's not here," Ben snapped. "So stop talking about him."

I knew Ben missed the gray stallion too, even if he acted like he was over our family's loss. Which he wasn't. None of us were.

El Cid had been our father's hunting partner before I was born. Dad even mentioned making a pilgrimage along a section of the *Camino del Cazador*—our ancestor's original route from Mexico to southern Colorado—in El Cid's memory. I hoped that included me and Ben.

"Too bad all the skinners are locked away." I spun my mace on its head between my boots. "Wouldn't mind a chance at some payback for what they did. Send 'em into oblivion. Permanently."

"It won't bring El Cid back."

"I know." I stared out my window. "But it might make me feel better."

"No, it won't." Ben shifted in his seat and did his own window-staring. "It'll still hurt. No matter how mad you get or how hard you hit, the dead stay dead."

I knew he wasn't thinking about El Cid.

"There's Dad."

I spied our father waiting across the street from the post office in the shade of the plaza's massive cottonwoods. At the sound of the truck's engine, he looked up from sorting through the mail, then smiled and tugged his hat brim at two women walking past. They glanced back, nudging each other.

Both Dad and Ben had inherited the Del Toro good looks. And they both knew it. Me? Not so much. At least, I didn't see it. Guess there was nothing left over in the gene pool when I came along. Dad always said I was a blend of him and our mother, Celia Montoya-Del Toro. She died when I was three and Ben was seven. Our father made sure there were pictures of her scattered throughout our house, in all of our bedrooms, and even a few pinned on the barn wall by the racks where we stored the saddles. Even though he missed her something awful, he made himself talk about her and tell us stories about her.

Except, lately he seemed to talk about Mom more easily. Like the sadness didn't tear him so much apart when he shared his memories. Maybe time did that—made the caverns in our hearts a little easier to visit. I hoped so.

With a nod, Ben drove past Dad and down the block, then made a U-turn, almost hitting another car. He waved an apology. "Listen, Matt. Do me a favor. Don't tell him about that woman. Okay? I need him in a good mood this afternoon."

"Why?"

"Going to ask him again about getting me a car," Ben said. "Round six of negotiations."

I groaned. "He'll kill me if he finds out I didn't let him know."

"Wait until later. Or even tomorrow. I mean, what's the rush? She's just another collector." He jabbed my shoulder. "C'mon. Help me out here."

"Fine. Okay." I sighed. "But you owe me. *Again.*"

"Thanks." He pulled over to the sidewalk, put the truck in neutral, and started to get out. Our father motioned him to stay put and opened the crew cab's back door.

"No, you drive." Dad climbed in. "There is a letter I am eager to read."

"What letter?" I sneaked a peek as we inched along with the rest of the afternoon traffic. Huerfano was the only town of decent size in these parts, so Saturdays were usually crammed with locals and tourists circling the plaza looking for a parking spot.

"This one." He held up a cream-colored envelope stamped with foreign postage. An ornate seal sporting a crown and flag decorated the upper left corner.

My heart kicked like a jack rabbit. I had to admit, knowing that His Royal Highness, King Felipe VI—yeah, *that* king, the current monarch of Spain—corresponded directly with our father was all kinds of cool

Pushing his hat back, Dad slid a pair of reading glasses from his shirt pocket and balanced them on his hawk-like nose. He tore open the envelope with a rip and unfolded the letter, face intent as he read silently.

"Well? Is it good news?" Holding my breath, I crossed my toes inside my boots.

"It is." Dad leaned forward and waved the heavy sheet of stationery in the air between us. The same crown and flag seal adorned the top of the page. It even *smelled* official. "He approved the cost of living increase and apologized for not thinking of it himself. We will see the additional funds in next month's stipend."

Grinning, Ben and I elbowed at each other. Maybe trickle-down economics would work in our favor, too.

"Listen to this." Dad cleared his throat. "'And while we have stated this in the past,'" he read in a measured tone, translating the Spanish into English, "'please accept once again our heartfelt and eternal gratitude to you, your sons, and your loyal warhorses, for faithful service and undying devotion to the task set before you. While your country may never know of the four centuries of sacrifice by the Family Del Toro, as well as the other members of the Order of the Knights of the Coffer, both in the past and to this day, its citizens live in safety because of your steadfast vigilance.'"

Sure, the words sounded like lines from *The Lord of the Rings*, but I liked them. Made us seem... *noble*. And noble wasn't a label the world usually slapped on us.

"To society," Dad always joked, "we are more blue collar than blue blood."

While we Del Toros had settled in southern Colorado, other Knights of the Coffer and their families lived scattered across the American Southwest. There were the Navarres in northern New Mexico, the Montoya clan down in Arizona, and the Reyes' wild bunch out in Utah, as well as others spread across parts of Texas and California. All of them even now secretly guarding centuries-old iron coffers filled with centuries-old monsters. All of them keeping those creatures from hurting or even killing innocent people. All fighting the good fight.

Yup. Noble.

"So, how much of an increase?" Ben asked. Trust my brother to get down to business. "Enough to get me a car?"

"Oh, *sí*."

The ease of Dad's answer flipped on my suspicion alarm. Our father never, ever folded that fast.

"Wait." Ben glanced in the rearview mirror. "You mean that? For real?"

"If you feel you must have one, my son."

I looked back too. Was he *really* going to break down and buy Ben his own car? Maybe that meant I'd get one when *I* was sixteen. Only four more years to go. I held my breath.

"Although," Dad folded the letter and slipped it back inside the envelope, "you both are due for dental check ups, Matt needs glasses, and—"

"Oh, no, I don't." I stomped down that stupid idea, even though, secretly, I agreed. Squinting into the distance wasn't doing it for me.

"—and Turk mentioned he could use a visit from the farrier sooner than later."

Ben rolled his eyes. "Why did I even bother asking?"

Scowling at the world, he broke free of the traffic and turned onto the street leading out of town. We drove past a row of small, weary houses. Out of habit, I glanced at Perry's. The Vandermer home sported a re-seeded lawn and a fresh coat of paint courtesy of us Del Toro men. A modest sized RV sat tucked into the side yard next to the house. Dust from the Maze still coated its windows.

Dr. Vandermer—a fossil expert who had grown up in Huerfano and had known our dad—had bought the rental house after deciding to move back permanently. Chicago's Field Museum of Natural History had offered her a job as the area's permanent—and only—resident paleontologist.

"Are you certain of this, Liz?" Dad had asked her one evening over supper at our place. "After what happened this summer? It is still dangerous, even with the skinners contained. We never know when one or more of those creatures will find a way to escape the coffer. Nothing is certain."

"True with everything in life, Javier," Dr. Vandermer had said with a shrug. "Look. I know the risks. I was there when those things attacked our camp, remember? And it's not like I'm going to establish another site *inside* the Maze. Learned my lesson. No, we'll stay *outside* the walls— plenty of fossils there to keep us busy for years." Her blue eyes had narrowed. "And, by the way, *you're* one to talk when it comes to questionable career choices. But this is my dream job and I already said yes, please, and how soon can I start. Not much of a salary, and I'm going to be spending this first year traveling a lot to secure more funding. But I didn't go into paleontology for the money. Nobody does. It's enough for Perry and me to live on."

"I'd live in a tent if it means staying here," Perry had added, one cheek bulging from an enormous bite of Dad's famous green chili cheeseburgers. "Heck, I'd go live in the Maze."

"Aren't you scared of those meatloaf mutts?" Ben had asked Perry. "Little kids are their favorite snack, you know."

Chewing, Perry had pointed a French fry at him. "Then you best stay out of there, too."

Rolling past the dead end sign on the edge of town, Ben sped up. He noticed me peeking back at Perry's house. "Awww, what's the matter? Missing your sweetie already? Wasn't she just over at our house yesterday?"

I rolled my eyes. "Why don't you come up with something different—that one's getting old. Perry's my *friend*. Guys and girls can be friends, you know."

"Yeah. Right. And Turk gives pony rides to little kids at the state fair."

"Speaking of Perry." Dad reached forward and biffed Ben on the back of the head. "Do not forget to clean your room before she arrives tomorrow. Change the sheets, too."

"Dang, I forgot." He made a face. "How long again?"

"Ten days." I wasn't sure how I felt about Perry staying with us while her mom was in Chicago doing whatever fossil experts did when they weren't fossilizing. On one hand, it meant I had to share a room with Ben so Perry could have his. But it also meant the four of us—me, Perry, and the horses—would get to hang out longer. Izzie was counting the days.

"Perry should just sleep out here with you," I joked yesterday, forking clean straw into the sorrel's corner of the barn.

"I told Javier that was our plan." Izzie tested the pile with a hoof. "But he said no. Killjoy."

With dust billowing behind and the afternoon sun nailing us in the eyes, we bounced along the three-mile dirt road toward home. Ahead of us, the Sangre de Cristo Mountains were a blue-gray battlement; the range sheltered our ranch from the worst of the winter storms roaring in from the west. Every peak was as familiar to me as my own toes. Old friends, they were.

Halfway home, something not so friendly pulled my focus northward. I squinted at the Maze, trying to see if anyone—or anything—moved in the Gate's dark shadow. Or worse, had gotten past the wards.

As El Cid used to say, evil had a way of leeching out.

Nearing home, we slowed and rounded a low hill, a distinctive one we called the Buffalo's Hump, which partially blocked our view of the Maze and the road to town. Not that we got any traffic since our ranch was the reason the dead-end road, well, *dead-ended*.

Gravel crunching under the tires, we pulled into the open yard between our small wooden ranch-style house and the large barn and stopped. The dust cloud caught up with the truck and crowded around us in a thick haze.

But it didn't hide the sight of Turk and Rigo going after each other in one muck-ugly horse fight.

Rearing, the stallions hammered at each other with their front hooves, bared teeth snapping like pit bulls. Dust and grunts and squeals of rage filled the air.

Stunned by their ferocity, I stared slack-jawed as Rigo dropped to earth, then whirled around and mule-kicked at the black stallion's nose. Turk wrenched his head out of range, mane flying. With a scream, he charged, using his heavier body as a battering ram. Rigo corkscrewed and skipped away, a brown jackrabbit.

Flinging the door open, Dad leaped out. "The hose. Hurry."

Ben and I scrambled from the truck and bolted for the barn. Hands fumbling, I grabbed the garden hose next to the horses' water barrel, shook the coils loose, then threw the nozzle at Ben. "Get ready!" I cranked the faucet on full. *Please let this work.*

Water blasted out of the end. Ben twisted the sprayer until the jet was needle-sharp. He aimed it at the stallions, stinging their flanks and chests with short bursts. I raced over and joined him.

"Hey! Don't point it at their faces." I snatched at the hose. "You'll hurt their eyes."

Ben knocked my arm away. "I know what to do. Stop yanking on it—Dad! Get out of there!"

I gasped at Ben's warning shout, my heart lodged in my throat.

Hollering and waving his arms, our father was smack in the middle of the brawl. His shouts were drowned out by the stallions' grunts and meaty thuds as hooves found targets. Ducking under Rigo's flailing front hooves, Dad lost his hat—and almost the top of his skull—as he lunged for Turk. Seizing the mane high on the black stallion's powerful neck, he grasped it with both hands, then braced his feet and pulled. "Turk," he shouted. "Enough!"

Turk ignored him. Screaming with fury and eyes white-rimmed crazy, he reared again. Dad's feet left the ground. Rigo danced on his hind legs and struck, almost nailing our father.

"Rigo, no!" I sprinted toward my war-brother. As his hooves touched earth, I flung my arms around his neck and grabbed his mane. My fingers slipped off the soaked strands. Crouching lower, I planted my shoulder and shoved as hard I could, boots skidding on the gravel. It was like trying to shift the barn off its foundation. "Knock it off."

"If you mean his head," Rigo paused, blowing hard and ears pinned flat, "then give me some room." He glowered at Turk through his dripping forelock. "The jerk started it. I was just bringing it home."

"If that's all you got, pony boy," Turk panted, "then it proves me right." He let loose twin blasts of mucus and water, then curled his lip. "Matt took a step back when he partnered with you."

"That is not true, Turk, and you know it." Dad let go of the stallion's mane and shook out his hands. "Stop baiting Rigo."

The black ignored him. "Not that El Cid was all that special," he continued. "The old goat just got good press. But still. For Matt to go from *him* to *you*." He snorted.

Rigo swelled.

I threw an arm across his chest. "Forget him. He's just messing with you." I tried to ignore a new concern creeping up on me: Did Rigo really think I considered him second string? Nope. No way. Not even a little.

Did he think I compared him to El Cid? Now, *that* question, I wasn't so sure about.

Dad glanced about. "Where is my hat?" Spying it, he snatched it out of the dust, slapped against his leg, then settled it back on his head, glaring at the stallions the whole time. "So. A second fight this week. Why all this hostility?"

Rigo flared his nostrils but said nothing. The earlier drenching, mixed with sweat, had darkened his coat from a rich mahogany to a deep walnut. Turk stood with his head raised and chest puffed out, eyes half hidden by the dripping forelock that hung almost to his nostrils in true Andalusian fashion.

"Well?" Dad folded his arms across his chest. "I am waiting."

In spite of the brawl, Ben and I grinned at each other. Dad sounded so much like, well, *Dad* when he caught us wrestling in the house or doing something we shouldn't.

"It's nothing, Javier," Turk said after a minute.

"Yeah. Nothing," Rigo added.

One of Dad's eyebrows lifted into a black question mark. "Much sound and fury for *nothing*. And where is Isabel? I am surprised she is not here in the thick of things, making matters worse."

Ben blinked. "Good question." He whistled shrilly between his teeth. "Izzie. Hey, Izzie!" he bellowed. Dad and the horses winced.

I turned off the hose and coiled it back up. Sort of.

Rigo and Turk pricked up their ears. A minute later, I caught the distant thunder of hooves. The one-two-three drumming grew louder, then Izzie loped around the corner of the barn. She slowed to a trot, breathing lightly.

"I told you guys to wait until I got back. Now, look. I missed the party." She shook her blonde forelock out of her eyes and studied the stallions. "I'd ask who won, but it looks like neither of you two outlaws. Bummer. I was hoping to take on the winner."

Ben patted her shoulder. "You better not, Izzie, you might hurt 'em. And we still need them."

"For *what*?" Rigo snorted, spraying me with watery slime. "Not like there's a lot of beastie bashing going on around here."

Great. Another worry crowded the earlier one: Did Rigo regret joining our family after El Cid died? I thought the bay stallion was happy. That he already felt at home with us, even though it had been less than two months. Maybe he had hoped for more monster hunting and less family drama. Guess we failed him in *both* of those arenas.

"Look, Rigo. I know it's kind of boring around here." I watched Dad and Turk speaking in low tones, my father examining a cut on his hunting partner's shoulder. "Sorry about that."

"Hey, I'm not blaming *you*, just stating a fact. I know the situation could change in an Albuquerque minute. And, by the way." Rigo nosed the side of my head. "Enough already. You're going to wear a hole in your skull stressing about something that's never going to happen."

"What do you mean?"

"You're worried that I'll change my mind about all this. About you and me teaming up. That one day soon, I'll hit the trail for the bright lights of somewhere else. Am I right?"

I kicked a rock toward the barn. "Well…"

"Well, nothing. It's not how I roll." He chuffed. "Heck, I can't leave now—I just got you house broken."

Laughing, I leaned back against his chest. Even wet, he felt warm and solid. I started to say something more. Before I could, my father waved us over.

"Perhaps we need to find a new way to stay sharp. Especially you, my friends." Dad pinned the horses with a bird of prey stare. "Because fighting amongst yourselves is not acceptable. One of you might become injured, just when we have need of our war-brothers. And, yes, our war-sister," he added, one beat ahead of Izzie's protest. "We cannot pursue skinners on foot. You know this."

"But those Chucky chuck roasts are all in storage," Ben said. "How can we keep up our training… Wait a minute."

His eyes widened. "You're not going to let them out, are you?"

"No, no, I am not *that* desperate. Yet."

I scratched my head. "Can you even open a coffer once it's sealed?" I eased away from Rigo with a pat. Between his wet coat and the afternoon sun, I was starting to feel like I was in a sauna.

"Oh, *sí*," Dad said. "After all, the coffers do us hunters little good if we cannot add to them as needed. And fortunately, *unsealing* is much easier, and less painful, than sealing."

"How?"

Ben frowned. "Didn't Allbury just pry the smaller one open with a tire iron or something?"

I noticed Rigo and Izzie were listening. Turk, too, even though he pretended he wasn't. The black did aloof better than anyone.

"The professor was able to open the coffers only because it had been years since they were last re-sealed," Dad said. "I am guessing the seals, or the chests themselves, have been failing for quite some time. That would explain the increase in the skinner population we had earlier this summer. However, now that both our coffers are tightly secured, it is almost impossible for anyone to open them. Only *our* maces have the magic and the power to break the seals. At least, for now."

"So, what's the trick?" I asked.

"A hard strike to the lid's corner or edge," Dad mimicked a swing with an imaginary weapon, "with one of our maces."

I waited. So did Ben. Was there more? Some magical words or a spell? A-once-in-a-century alignment of the stars and moon? Maybe a chicken sacrifice? "And?"

"And the blow should crack the seal. The lid will then open. Simple, no?"

Ben screwed up his face. "That's *it*? Just whack it and pop goes the coffer?"

Dad shrugged. "I am sorry it is not more dramatic."

A low grumble, barely on the edge of my hearing, snagged my attention. It grew louder. I craned my neck and squinted toward the road. *Dang. Dad may be right about glasses after all.* A cloud of dust rose from the Hump's far side and turned it into a mini-volcano. Ears pricked, Rigo edged around me, bumping me to one side.

"Turk?" Dad gestured toward the road. "Who is it?"

"Not a vehicle *I'm* familiar with. Don't even think it's a truck or a car." The stallion cocked his head. "Sounds like a hog. Or a chopper. Big one, too."

Hog? Chopper? My lungs stopped working, along with my mouth. I forced the words out. "Y-you mean like a... a *motorcycle*?"

Oh, boy.

With a growl, a motorcycle appeared around the Hump. It rumbled toward us, shaking the ground and dragging a cloud of dust. Big and heavy and tricked out with lots of flashy chrome, it sported a pair of oversized saddlebags that straddled the back wheel. The rider, clad in a leather jacket and workman's boots, wove smoothly around potholes and tire ruts. Even though the features were hidden by a full-face helmet, I knew who the rider was.

Ben glanced at me. "Is that…?"

I nodded. Dang, but she gave me the creeping creeps. Maybe it was her size. Or the fact that she had tracked us down so fast. I wondered who in town squealed.

And, why, why, why didn't I tell Dad about her earlier? *Because I hate it when he's in a bad mood. And because I'm a stupid idiot to listen to Ben.*

The bike slowed, then halted at the edge of the yard near the ruins of the adobe walls that marked our family' original homestead. Face still hidden, the rider killed the engine. For a long moment, she sat there, legs braced on either side of the machine. The only sound was the engine's ticking and the low hum of a few horseflies. Turk snapped once, chewed, then swallowed. Yeesh.

She reached up and pulled off her helmet. Her white hair had lost some of its spikiness. Hooking a heel on the kickstand, she lowered it, then swung a leg over and dismounted. The whole time, her ice-blue eyes swept the area.

Rigo circled his nose in the air, nostrils and mouth working like he had caught a whiff of something gross. Lowering his head, he hooked his chin over my shoulder and drew me closer to his side.

My pulse sped up. "What's wrong?" I whispered.

Before he answered, Turk marched forward, steel shoes pinging on the gravel and upper lip curled tightly. Guess he didn't like the stranger's smell, either.

"Wait." Dad motioned him back, then removed his hat. "Good afternoon. May I help you?"

"You'd be the first one in a long while." She rested the helmet on one of the saddle bags, then hooked an elbow on the handlebars. "Although I guess Allbury counts. A little. He gave me just enough information to narrow down my search before he vamoosed into hiding."

At the mention of Allbury, I cringed. She *was* another collector. Who knew seventeenth-century iron chests were such hot commodities? Still, if folks knew what were *inside* those chests, they might not be so eager beaver to acquire them. Heck, Allbury barely escaped with his life after stealing ours. If it hadn't been for me and Rigo being in the right place at the right time, something Brothers Grimm would've crawled out of the smaller one and killed him. That sure would've taught the guy a lesson about taking stuff that didn't belong to him.

Head cocked, she eyed my father, taking in his mud-splattered jeans and boots. "So, you're the famous Francis Javier Del Toro. Wow. You're older than I thought you'd be. Shorter, too. But don't take that as an insult. I say it to everyone."

"I am sorry." Dad tapped his hat against his leg. "But if you are here because of misinformation from Dr. Allbury—"

"And these must be your sons. I heard you had two. An heir and a spare, as the saying goes." Her gaze flicked from me to Ben before glancing around. "Can't say I'm all that impressed with your place. Not how I imaged the legendary hunter and monster slayer would live." A pale eyebrow rose. "Unless you're slumming it? You know. To keep a low profile?"

I stiffened, ordering my face to stay blank. Hard to do when my skull was whirling like a blender. How much did she know about us? Did she know about the warhorses? The other Knights? Who told her?

"*Monsters*?" Dad laughed and shook his head. "If this is a joke, it is a poor one."

"Nice try, Javier. Mind if I call you Javier? Fits you better than *Francis*, that's for sure. You're too good-looking a man to be a saint."

I gagged. Bad enough this Looney Tune loon—who knew about monsters and who we *really* were—had stalked us to our place. Now she was making verbal passes. At my father. Double yeesh.

"You can drop the clueless routine," she said. "I know about you hunters. Or to use your more *official* titles, Knights of the Coffer. And, wow, did it take awhile to find you—folks are sure ziplocked lipped when it comes to you people. That includes your little Disney menagerie. Yeah, I heard about your chatty ponies." She wiggled her fingers at the warhorses. "Feel free to speak up anytime. I know you can."

Turk did just that. "What'd you want?"

"*El Cofre Rojo.*" She rolled the name around with a dramatic flair. "Or should I say, the Red Casket. I'm willing to negotiate on the price."

At her mention of the smaller casket hidden in the Maze, my damp shirt went from clammy to chilly. I shivered. Who *was* this person? Really? And why'd she want the Red Casket? Didn't she know there was something trapped inside?

Of course she knew.

"Word on the street is you've got it hidden," she poked a thumb northward over her shoulder, "somewhere in the Maze."

Rigo lowered his head. "*Bruja,*" he breathed, his whiskers prickling my ear.

I gasped. "You mean she's a... *witch*?" Oops. That came out a little louder than I intended.

"Which old witch?" Izzie said promptly.

"The wicked witch." Ben didn't miss a beat.

Dang, but I loved my family.

"Watch your mouth, kid." She laid a stinkeye on me. "I'm a *sorceress*. We're the ones who make witches and wizards step back and take a number."

"A sorceress." Dad replaced his hat. Guess he decided certain supernatural folks weren't worthy of old-fashioned manners. "That is quite a claim, as is the history behind it. You know I will not have any dealings with your kind. And I will certainly never hand over one of our coffers."

Man, was I glad to hear Dad take that stand. Rigo and I had only gotten a brief look of what was in the Red Casket. And that glimpse was one too many.

A cloud of smoke billowing out to envelop me. Only it doesn't feel like smoke. It feels wet and clammy. Like fog or rain. And the smell—moldy leaves or the muddy bottom of a puddle drying under a July sun. The stench clogs my nostrils. With a soft hiss, the cloud coils around my head once, leaving my cheeks wet, then shoots toward the mountains and out of sight.

Before I can draw a clean breath, something else moves inside the chest. A hand, with twiggy fingers and bark-like flesh, curls over the coffer's lip and twitches against the latch. How could a box so small hold something the size of a human? Worse, is it alone?

The hand retreated until only the tips of split and broken nails showed. Had the thing tried to claw its way out?

I shuddered at the memory. It didn't help that another member of Team Creepy was currently standing in the middle of our yard.

"I know what you're thinking, Javier," the sorceress said. "But whatever *was* inside is long gone, dead and dusted. I simply want the remains, that's all. To make good on a promise, you might say. So you can throttle back on your righteous attitude toward me because there's nothing dangerous or threatening, or even valuable, inside that chest. Trust me."

"We Knights never trust a *bruja*. We learned that lesson centuries ago."

She sighed. "Does that mean no, you won't sell it to me?"

"It does. This conversation is over. Now get off my land."

The sorceress nodded. "Yeah, I figured you'd be this way. Guess we're going to have to take negotiations in a new direction." With a wild grin, she reached inside her jacket.

"Heads up," Rigo shouted. "She's packing!"

Shoving past, my war-brother planted his body between me and the threat. Izzie clamped down on my brother's shirt with her teeth and yanked him backwards. Ben yelped. Guess Izzie got some skin along with the T-shirt.

I stood on tiptoe, trying to see over Rigo. "Dude, move," I hissed.

"Not on your life. Literally. You just stay put."

I gave up and peeked under his neck.

Turk waited at Dad's shoulder. His whole body seemed to swell like a cobra's hood, spitting mad and ready to strike. I wondered if the sorceress knew she was one bad move from having eleven hundred pounds of Andalusian go off on her.

Apparently, she didn't know. Or didn't care. She whipped her hand out of the jacket and raised her arm. Rigo tensed. I flinched, shoulders hunched and breath caught in my chest.

Then, I blinked in surprise. "What the heck?"

"Is she threatening us," Rigo huffed in disbelief, "with a *stick*?"

I peered more closely. About the length of my forearm, but not as thick, the knobby stick twisted around itself. A pointy yellow crystal inserted into its tip reminded me of a lame Harry Potter meets Gandalf mashup. "I think… I think it's a *wand*."

"Huh." Rigo clopped his lips. "Didn't know those things were real."

"That's what a lot of folks think," the sorceress said. "Right up to the moment I blast a hole through them." She flicked her wrist. Almost instantly, the crystal began to glow with a mucus-y yellow light. She aimed it straight at Dad.

Oh, crud, my mace! For the second time that afternoon, I realized I had left my weapon in the truck. Worse, so had my father and brother. Pulse hammering, I began inching sideways, one eye on the sorceress. *Get to the truck. Grab a mace. Toss it to Dad.*

"You make one more move, Matt," Rigo growled, "and I'll pin your foot to the ground. Turk's got Javier's back. See?"

Right on cue, the black warhorse stomped closer and took up battle position, legs braced, neck arched, and tail lashing from side to side. "Keep pointing that thing at Javier and you'll be picking crystal out of your teeth. If you *have* any teeth after I plant a hoof in your face."

"Wow." The sorceress sighed, then shook her head. "Okay, gotta tell you, as threats go, that one was kind of weak." The sorceress raised the crystal higher. "If I were you, big guy, I'd duck."

The crystal's glow swelled, growing brighter each second. Eyes watering, I squinted, one hand braced on Rigo's neck. His hide was drumhead tight.

KAA-RACK!

A blob of yellow light shot out. About the size of a baseball, the fireball hurtled past Turk's head, singeing his mane. It slammed into the side of the barn. *BAM!* Sparks flew. They drifted to the wet ground and died with a sizzling protest. I stared open-mouthed at the hole big enough to put my fist through.

The sorceress aimed the crystal again. *KAA-RACK!* Another blast. Now the hole in the barn was big enough for my head. Embers outlined the gap in the dried wood for a moment, then faded.

The only one who hadn't flinched was Dad. Naturally.

"The obligatory warning shots?" My father's cool tone didn't match his fisted hands.

The sorceress nodded. "A live demo goes a long way. That said." She lowered the weapon and pointed it at the ground. "I don't want to come across as a burro's south end. I've got standards. So let's deal. I'll pay you market price for the casket. Black market, that is. Cash. Small bills. From the looks of things around here, you could use the money. I'll even give you three days. Plenty of time to go dig it up or open the vault or whatever and haul it back here."

"How much cash?" Ben asked. Our father shot him a look over his shoulder. "What? I was just asking."

Dad turned back and raised his chin. "Three days. Three years. Three centuries. The answer will be no. As I said earlier, I never trust a witch."

"Sorceress," she reminded him. "And the clock is now ticking." She held up three fingers.

"Oh, look," Izzie said. "She can count."

Turk sniffed. "Just on one hand."

With the crystal's haft clamped under an arm, the sorceress pulled on her helmet and started the bike. Revving the engine to a painful scream, she wheeled the big hog around in a spray of dirt and gravel and roared away, leaning low over the handlebars. We watched as she disappeared behind the Hump, then re-appeared on the dirt road toward town. A cloud of dust and exhaust chased after her.

My knees decided they were done for the day. I slumped against Rigo, heart punching my ribs, then slid down his leg until I hit the ground.

Dad spun on a heel and marched over to the truck. Face a thunderstorm and lips pressed wire-thin, he yanked the door open, pulled out Ben's mace and tossed it to him, then grabbed his own and mine. "Until this is over, keep your weapons with you at all times." He slammed the door and held out my mace. "Starting now."

"Going out on a limb here." Ben looped the haft's leather strap around his wrist. "But I'm guessing she's *not* an antique collector."

"Not even close," Rigo said. "Especially if she's who I think she is."

"You know about her?" Sure, I was stalling, because I knew Dad would boot me into the middle of next week for not warning him earlier.

"A little." The stallion lowered his head and nudged me. "Grab on."

The bay's black mane draped like a curtain along his neck. Reaching up, I snagged a fistful and held tight. He lifted his head, pulling me to my feet in one smooth move.

I let go and flexed my fingers. "So? Who is she?"

Rigo flattened his ears. "Javier?"

"*Sí?*" Dad quirked an eyebrow.

"We've got a problem."

7

"Her name is Hester Lemprey," Rigo announced over the banging of hammers.

Hips cocked, he and the other horses relaxed in the shade near the porch. Lucky them. The lack of opposable thumbs had its benefits from time to time. *I* was stuck working under a mean summer sun, repairing the *bruja*-blasted siding on the barn. Yup, the fun never stopped around our ranch. Dad held the boards in place while I pounded nails. Sweat soaked my hair and trickled down my face and stung my eyes.

Pausing to catch my breath, I blew a drip from my nose. "How do you know her?"

"The Montoyas mentioned her when I was at their ranch last year helping out with that infestation of sand demons." Rigo shifted his hind legs and cocked his other hip. "Victoria said she'd heard about some woman the size of a Viking refrigerator who had been nosing around. Asking the locals about the Montoyas and if they had any antique chests in their possession. Offered big dollars for any information. And you know Victoria, Javier."

Dad dragged a sleeve across his face. "She did some research. Called her sources and contacts."

Rigo nodded. "Victoria has an underground network that puts the CIA to shame. She found out this stranger wasn't just your average *bruja*—she was packing a powerful crystal with a heck of a kick. Before the Montoyas could confront her, Hester Lemprey went to ground. No one's caught a whiff of her since."

"Until today," Izzie said over her shoulder. Standing side by side and head-to-hindquarters with Rigo, she whisked a fly off the bay's face with a flick of her tail. "It's got to be the same woman."

Arms full of lumber, Ben stepped out of the barn. "And I bet she's already been asking around Huerfano about us." He dropped the replacement boards by my feet with a crash. "Don't you think, Matty?"

I sneered at both the stupid nickname and the not-so-subtle hint. Since I knew my brother wouldn't cowboy up and tell our father, I took a deep breath. "Dad?"

"Matt." He picked up a board, eyed it lengthwise, then tossed it to one side and selected another one.

"I, uh..." I cleared my throat. "Ben's right. Hester Lemprey *was* in Huerfano earlier."

"*Sí*, I know. She rode past me while I was waiting for you two."

My jaw sagged. So did Ben's. "W-why didn't you tell us?"

"Because at the time, I did not know who or what she was." Our father paused and looked up from the board. "And when did *you* see her?"

"At the 7-Eleven. She was asking about you."

Dad's face darkened. "And you chose not to inform your brother or me about such a stranger? What were you thinking?"

I hated the "what were you thinking" question. It always meant I hadn't. "Um…"

"Mateo Del Toro, you are smarter than this." He threw the plank on the ground. It hit the pile with a clatter. "You know our lives depend on making good decisions. And this was a poor one on your part."

My heart sank to my boot heels. Behind Dad, my brother shrugged. *Sorry*, he mouthed.

No way was I taking the fall alone. Sure, it went against the code of brothers, but hey, I was desperate. "I *did* tell Ben. He said not to tell you. That you'd go ballistic about another collector showing up."

Dad planted his fists on his hips. "And if he told you to leap from the barn's roof, would you?"

Yeah, sure, Dad. I'd climb right up and do that very thing. You bet. "'Course not."

"Then, next time, stop and think before taking someone's advice. You must rely on your own judgment. Always do the right thing even if it is difficult. *Comprende?*"

"*Sí, Papá.*" Indignation sputtered inside of me, then burst into flame. Why wasn't he jumping on Ben's case as well? Why was he just picking on *me*?

"One day, you will be the one everyone depends upon, Matt. Listen to those you trust, yes, but do not let them down because you took the easy way out and did not think for yourself."

Fuming inside, I nodded, then shot a glare at my brother. *See if I ever help* you *out again, you smear of roadkill.*

"And Rueben?"

"*Sí, Papá?*"

Dad narrowed his eyes.

"Just kidding." Ben raised his hands in surrender. "And, yeah. My bad. I should've let you know about her. At least not stopped Matt from telling. That said." He hesitated, then continued. "Why not sell her the Red Casket? One less coffer for us to worry about *and* we'd make some money from the deal. Win-win."

"Are you kidding?" I said, stunned by Ben's suggestion. "More like lose-lose. There's something inside the coffer. Rigo and I saw it, remember? And since that witch Hester Lamper wants it so much—"

"Lemprey," Rigo said.

"—Hester *Lemprey* wants it so much, then what's inside should *stay* inside."

"I agree," Dad said. "Matt, describe the creature again. Do not leave out any details."

Eye half closed, I visualized the scene. "Well, there was this hand. Human sized, but like a mummy's or zombie's. You know, with dried up skin. It tried to crawl out. I showed it my mace, told it to back off, then recited that Latin phrase you taught us. Then, *bam*—the blast sealed the lid and knocked me out cold." I opened my eyes. "Did I forget anything, Rigo?"

"The fog. Now, there's a stench I'll never forget." He wrinkled his nose. "Like a century's worth of stored-up farts. It disappeared right after that idiot Allbury opened the lid." He huffed. "But, Javier, I kind of agree with Ben. Let her have the coffer. Matt welded it shut good and tight. Since folks can't simply pry it open like Allbury did, what's the harm?"

"Who cares why she wants it or what's inside?" Turk shivered away a horsefly feeding on the wound on his shoulder. "We need to plan what to do when she shows up here again. Although I'm still game for planting a hoof in her face."

"Oh, sure," Izzie muttered. "Give her *another* barn to hit."

Turk flattened his ears. "What's that supposed to mean?"

"It means," Rigo jumped in, "that you're as big as a building and about as nimble."

As the horses began slinging insults—Izzie was a Kentucky Derby champion at it—my mind drifted back to those few moments when the Red Casket's lid was open. Something I noticed and couldn't stop thinking about.

It was the hand's fingernails. Talon-like, they were black and chipped and broken; some were even peeled off. And the inside of the lid had been decorated with what looked like scratches, hundreds of lines of brighter silver in the aged iron. I shuddered. Had the creature tried to claw its way out?

I would if I had been trapped in there.

Ever since I could remember, I hated tight, confined places. Just the thought of being imprisoned inside that small box made my palms break out into a sweat and my stomach twist into knots of barbed wire. Hands down, my worst nightmare.

Maybe that creature felt the same way.

S lumped in a corner of our worn-out sofa and my head stuffed full of questions and worries, I waited while Dad finished in the kitchen; it was his night for dishes. Ben had disappeared right after supper, declaring he needed to spend some quality time with the truck's engine. Restless, I used the end of my mace to poke bits of foam back into the holes of the frayed material.

When Dad said to keep our weapons with us, he meant literally touching some part of our bodies at all times. I'd probably even have to sleep with it.

Done with upholstery duty, I balanced the mace across my knees. The haft's leather wrapping was stained from age and sweat and skinner remains and needed a good cleaning and some oil. A leather loop hung from the handle. The iron ball—a little bigger than my fist—was decorated on four sides with our family's sigil: a crescent moon, its tips curved upward like the horns of a bull. A shallow gouge marked where I had missed a skinner on a hunt earlier in the summer and nailed a boulder instead. Another battle scar to add to the weapon's collection.

Centuries of monster walloping had sure done a number on those Del Toro moons, even though they were etched deeply into the iron. They were still there, though.

Faithful service and undying devotion to the task set before you…

Dang right.

Dad walked into the room, drying his hands on his jeans. His mace was tucked under one arm.

I straightened. "So, what are we going to do? When she comes back. Since we're not handing over the coffer, how are we going to stop her from frying us?"

"I have some ideas." He sat down in one of the recliners, propped his weapon in easy reach next to him, then toed off his boots.

I thought about the fireballs the sorceress had shot. Their speed and power. What the bolts would do to one of us. Or one of the horses. Anxiety churned the three helpings of mac and cheese in my gut. I curled a fist around my mace. "Too bad we can't stuff *her* inside the Red Casket. See how she likes being trapped…"

The rest of my words died as the mother of all questions took a seat beside me. I gasped. How had I missed the obvious? "Why didn't she just grab it herself?"

"Hester Lemprey?"

"Yeah. Why hasn't she stolen the casket already?" I scooted forward and perched on the edge of the sofa. "If Allbury told her about the coffers, I bet he also told her they were hidden in a cave in the Maze. Probably gave her the cave's GPS location and everything. Not that a GPS unit would work in there. Heck, our phones barely do." The words spilled out of my mouth in a jumble as details occurred to me. "But even so, he could've described the cave's location well enough. So, why doesn't she just go in there and take it? She doesn't need *us* to bring it out."

"Why do you think?" Dad leaned back, hands clasped behind his head. "In other words, what is preventing one such as Hester Lemprey from entering the Maze?"

Jiggling my feet, I chewed on the inside of my cheek. I felt like I should know. Like the answer was dancing in front of me and waving its arms. "Do *you* know?"

"I have a theory." He waited.

"Going to share it?"

"After you, my son. Consider this a lesson in understanding the enemy's strengths and weaknesses."

"Well, either she tried and couldn't find the cave. Or she couldn't—Oh!" I jumped to my feet. My mace tumbled from my lap and landed with a clunk. I snatched it up. "The wards!"

"What about the wards?"

"Well." I paced across the room to Dad's desk in the corner and back again. "She made a big deal out of being a sorceress, right?"

"She did."

"So, is she, you know, *human*?"

Dad thought for a moment. "From what I have read and heard, a sorcerer or sorceress must trade their humanity— their *soul*, in a way—in return for powers and abilities like we saw today. While she may retain a sliver of humanity, most hunters would classify Hester Lemprey as a supernatural or magical being." He cocked his head. "So?"

"So, if she's supernatural—nonhuman—then maybe the wards are stopping her from getting *inside* the Maze. Just like they stop the skinners—also nonhuman—from getting *out*." I held my breath, hoping it didn't sound as stupid as I thought it did.

"Ah, Matt." Dad smiled. "It seems you have inherited my brains after all."

"Does that mean I'm right?"

"I think so, but we will not know until she makes an attempt. I wish there was a way to test our theory. In the meantime, we must focus on how to defeat her." He sighed. "While I dislike waiting for her to bring the fight to us, it is better than battling in the streets of Huerfano."

"True that."

Rising, my father picked up his mace and took a stance in the middle of the living room. A frown pinched his brows as he examined the weapon. "Hmm."

"I don't think our maces will work on those lightning bolt, fireball thingies she shot at us." I plopped back down on the sofa and braced my feet on the coffee table until he gave me the "boots off the furniture" look.

"Our maces have been effective against all kinds of evil for centuries." Dad picked something off the head of his mace with a thumbnail and flicked it away. "They have yet to fail us."

"Fireballs aren't monsters. You can't just... *whack* 'em like we do skinners."

"Why not? The bolts were about the size of a baseball, no?" Gripping the haft in both hands, he cocked it over his right shoulder and took a slow practice swing.

"They also have the *speed* of a baseball." My eyes widened. "Wait. Are you saying we can simply *bat* them away? Dad, that's crazy."

"*Muy loco*," he agreed. "But crazy can be a good strategy from time to time." He swung again, faster. "As a hunter, you must sometimes think outside of the box when forced to make the call."

"How do you know if you've made the right one?"

He shrugged. "Sometimes, my son, there is no right or wrong decision. There is only the best decision you can make at the time. But, as I told you earlier, listen to those you trust. A leader leads, but they also consult others. It is a balancing act."

A thump of boots echoed from the porch. Ben walked in, wiping his hands on some paper towels and mace dangling from his wrist. The screen whapped shut behind him. "I know why the truck is stalling out all the time. The distributor cap is about shot."

Scowling, Dad lowered his weapon. "Replaceable?"

"Yeah. But I'll need some help. I'll see if Lee's folks," Ben named one of his friends, "will let me work on it at their repair shop. Means you won't have a vehicle tomorrow. See, another reason for us to have a second car."

"Even with the increase next month," Dad said, "we simply do not have that kind of money. I am sorry."

"I know where to get some." Ben wadded up the oily towels and tossed them on the coffee table, then perched on the arm of the sofa.

"You mean sell the coffer to Hester Lemprey." Our father frowned. "Do you not remember what we discussed earlier? We cannot take the risk that she might use whatever is inside to harm people."

"Look, don't take this the wrong way, but we can't guard every person from every monster," Ben said. "I don't see why it's always up to us to save the day."

I loved my brother something fierce, but sometimes I wondered how we could have the same DNA. I glanced at our father's face. Lines I never noticed before deepened.

"Do you really believe that?" Dad asked. "That we do not have a responsibility to make this world safer, not only for our friends, but for people we do not know? Especially when we have the power to do so?"

"'Because with great power comes great—'" I began. Dad shot me a look. I closed my mouth with a snap.

Ben huffed. "You make it sound like I don't care about... about *stuff* I should care about. I do, and I always will. But, c'mon. We have a right to live a normal life, too. Didn't you ever want something different than *this*?" He waved an arm around.

"I was not given the choice. However," Dad raised a hand, forestalling Ben's next words, "I do not regret this life."

"What about Matt? Did you give him the choice? Or did you tag him without asking him."

Our father ran a hand down his goatee; a faint blush crept across his cheekbones. He started to say something, then gave up and sighed. "I have not spoken to Matt about it. *Yet*. But you know what his answer will be as well as I do."

Ben glanced at me, then barked a short laugh. "He's such a Javier mini-me."

"What are you guys talking about?" I looked at Ben, then Dad, stomach roiling. Had I missed something? "What choice? What's going on?"

"Aw, you can't be *that* clueless. On the other hand, maybe you can." Ben's grin widened. "Congratulations, Mateo Del Toro. You are," he made quote marks in the air with his fingers, "'the Chosen One.'"

"*Chosen?*" My voice squeaked. "Chosen for what?"

"To take over the family business."

I sat bolt upright on the sofa. Talk about a kick in the skull. Ben was right—I *was* totally oblivious. Was that why Dad had lectured me about relying on my own judgment? When to take advice from others? The importance of understanding one's enemy?

"W-why *me*?" I swallowed around a mouth suddenly dry. "Why not Ben? Or Ben *and* me?"

"Because, while your brother wishes to do his part," Dad exchanged looks with Ben, who nodded, "he does not know what that part looks like. We both think he will not find it here."

"Wait." Cold dread shot through me as I stared at my brother. "Are you *leaving*?"

"Okay, before you start freaking, no, I'm not leaving," Ben said. "At least, not for awhile. Look, it's just something Dad and I've have been talking about."

Dad stepped closer and squeezed my brother's shoulder. "I have said this before, but always remember: It will never be too late to change your mind."

"I know, Pop. And I appreciate it. But Matt'll be better at it than I would." He slid out from under our father's hand and rose. "Better get to town before the Napa store closes. Make sure they have the parts."

I sat in silence until the grumble of the truck's engine died away. My head whirled; I clutched the armrest for support. Would I really be better at running things than Ben? Hunting skinners and taking care of the ranch. Making sure everyone stayed safe. Stayed alive.

Doing what we Del Toros have done for centuries.

A big part of my brain said nope, no way, and why couldn't my family just stay the way it was. A smaller, more secret, more honest part whispered heck, yeah, I would. *You knew Ben would leave one day*, the voice whispered. *Why are you so surprised?*

Something stirred inside of me, a bull pawing the ground before it charged. I didn't know how I felt about taking over the ranch—the idea was too big a load to hoist into the saddle with me right then. But I did know one thing: I would do whatever it took to keep my family safe. I wasn't going to lose anyone else.

My father took a seat beside me. "Are you all right?"

I shrugged. I didn't want to talk about it. Not yet. I needed time to adjust to this new horizon. "What's going on with Ben?" I asked instead.

He patted my knee, acknowledging the change in subject. "A Del Toro tradition I am attempting to change."

"What do you mean?"

"That brother of yours. In some ways, he is so like mine. Your Uncle Sebastian was also reluctant to be part of this family's mission. He left home as soon as he could."

"How old was he?" Rare for Dad to talk about his brother, so I scrambled for the opportunity to learn more.

"He was not quite eighteen. As you know, your grandparents died within months of each other. I do not think they ever got over your Aunt Cristina's death. First Papá, then Mamá. Sebastian left the day after we buried our mother."

"So, you were only..."

"I was nineteen."

Whoa. Nineteen years old and all alone on the ranch. Only the old warhorse, Catalina, for company. *Oh, Dad.*

"Do you ever hear from him? From Sebastian?"

Dad shifted in his seat. "Oh, he leaves voice messages a few times a year."

"What does he say?"

"I do not know. I delete them."

My throat tightened. "Will Ben do that? Just leave one day and we won't hear from him?" *That he'll call and you won't answer?*

"For many years, I resented Sebastian's decision." Dad stared through the screen door at the approaching dusk. I wondered what he was seeing. "But I should not have cut him from my life. *Our* lives. It is my fault that damage is done. However." He hooked an arm around my neck and patted my chest. "I will not make the same mistake with Ben. That is why I will not tie him down. If he wishes to run free, then I will unlatch the corral gate. And whenever he comes home, the door will be open. Always."

"No matter what?"

"No matter what, *mijo*."

"What if he does something stupid or gets in a tight spot or…" *Or he needs us.*

"Then I will go to him," Dad said. "When it comes to my sons, I am relentless."

"Promise?"

"Pinky swear." He held up his hand, littlest finger extended.

Laughing weakly, I pushed his arm away. "That's just so wrong."

He checked his watch, then rose with a grunt. "I need to call Liz. She may not want Perry here with a *bruja* skulking about."

"Kind of last minute for them to make other arrangements."

"*Sí*, I know." He sighed. "And I should also call the Montoyas. I need to learn more about sorceresses in general and this Hester Lemprey in particular."

"Have you asked Roman?" I thought about my dad's best friend and fellow hunter, Roman Navarre. Built like an offensive lineman, he rode a dappled gray warhorse, the stallion Vasco, as massive as he was. Ben and I always jokingly referred to the pair as the heavy cavalry. He, along with his wife, Kathleen, and their seventeen-year-old daughter Jo lived on the sprawling *Rancho de Navarre* that straddled the border between Colorado and New Mexico. "He might know about witches and all that."

"He and Kathleen are still in Ireland—their flight home is not until tomorrow. Or is it the day after? I cannot remember." Scrolling through his phone, he stepped around his desk and took a seat behind it, chair wheels squealing. "They so seldom get a chance to visit Kathleen's family, and I will not ruin their last few days unless it is absolutely necessary." He gestured toward the spare chair next to the desk. "I have a task for you."

"Is it boring?" I walked over and dragged the wooden chair closer. Its legs screeched in protest along the floor. I felt the same way.

Reaching behind him, Dad pulled a thick journal from the shelf. Crammed with loose, yellowed papers, its leather cover was worn from handling. A piece of string tied around it held everything in place. He untied it, pulled a handful of pages from it, then passed the rest of the bundle to me. "While I make my calls, read through my grandfather's journal for any information concerning *brujas* or sorceresses. Their powers, abilities. What weapons are effective against them. You know what to look for."

"Do I have to take notes?"

He smiled and slid a sheet of paper across the desk.

అంజ

Cross-eyed from skimming page after page covered in my great-grandfather's script-y handwriting, I slumped back with a sigh. The soft scratching of Dad's pen filled the room, along with the summer evening. I clicked on the desk lamp, then scrubbed my face and turned the next sheet. The edges of the dried paper disintegrated beneath my fingers. I blew the specks away.

A loose page slid free and landed on the floor. I picked it up. Slicker and newer than the others, it looked like it was torn from a catalog, the kind art museums sold in their gift shops. Tilting it toward the lamplight, I held it closer to my face.

It was a photograph of an oil painting, the colors dull and muted. A man in chain mail and helmet was mounted on a rearing horse in the courtyard of a castle. Right off, I recognized the breed. The arched neck, powerful hindquarters, and strong legs, along with a thick flowing mane and tail, were pure Andalusian. The man carried a shield on his left arm and wielded a mace in his right. I remembered telling Perry once the mace was as much a traditional weapon of mounted knights as a sword was.

A woman, face concealed by her cloak's hood, stood on a wall above the horse and rider. She grasped the golden collar of a wingless lion-sized dragon perched beside her on the parapet. Red flames, the same shade as the woman's cloak, spewed from the dragon's open mouth.

Baby Smaug, except it doesn't have any wings, I thought. *I've got to show this to Perry.*

Squinting, I read the tiny description in the lower right-hand corner. *Oil on canvas. Spain. Circa late 1700s. Painter unknown. The Metropolitan Museum of Art. New York, New York.*

I tried to imagine Mateo Francis Del Toro—my great-grandfather—wandering around the Big Apple in a cowboy hat and boots back in the mid-1950s. "Did your grandfather really go to New York?" I held out the page.

Dad peered at it over his reading glasses, then returned to his work. "No, a friend sent it to us. Papá stored it in the journal for safekeeping. He was very proud his forebearer was immortalized in a famous painting in such a museum."

"Forebearer?" I asked.

"Read the back."

I flipped it over. "Whoa."

The title, *Santiago Del Toro and the Wyrm of Avila*, jumped out at me. I thought about our ancestor, the legendary Santiago Del Toro, who had helped rid medieval Spain of a medieval assortment of monsters by locking them away in magical coffers, then journeyed to the New World to bury the chests in remote areas. We Del Toros have been in southern Colorado ever since, keeping the faith, keeping the watch, and keeping those skinners pinned inside the Maze.

Gazing at the photo again, I just made out the Del Toro moon on the Knight's shield. I glanced over my shoulder at our own black shield hanging above the fireplace mantle. Its pale crescent moon matched the one in the painting. "Too bad *our* shield isn't a real one. That'd be cool."

Dad paused and looked at me. "What are you talking about? Of course it is real. It is the shield of Santiago."

"Wait." I blinked. "Seriously? Like for *real* real? Why didn't you ever tell us?"

"Ben knows, so I assumed you did as well. In any case, why would we have displayed it so prominently if it was not so?"

"I didn't think it was genuine," I said. "I thought it was just a metal plaque or something with our sigil on it. You know. For decoration."

"Decoration." Dad lifted an eyebrow. "Like a... *wreath*?"

"Okay, not a decoration. More like when people hang a Denver Broncos' banner by their front door. Go Team Del Toro and all that."

The other eyebrow rose. "Team Del Toro."

"Stop repeating me." I huffed in exasperation. "You know what I mean."

He laughed, then nodded at the shield. "It is real, and yes, it *is* Santiago's own shield. Why do you think I am always yelling at you two to stop banging on it?"

"Thought the noise bugged you." I walked over to the fireplace, grateful to be moving, and studied the shield. A little bigger than my torso, it was shaped like a kite and slightly convex. I reached up and rapped it with my knuckles. As always, it rang like a gong. "Have you ever used it?"

"I have taken it down a few times to oil the leather grips on the back. But, no, I have not carried it into battle, if that is what you are asking. It becomes heavy quickly, and besides, it is not so useful as our maces, especially against skinners."

Nodding, I tapped it again. A soft *clang*. A whisper of an idea whisked through my head. Before I grabbed hold, it disappeared.

Something about the shield...

The day's events followed me to bed. Lying in the dark, my thoughts pinged around inside of my skull, ricocheting between the wicked witch's threats to the whole taking-over-the-ranch revelation. After an hour of twisting my covers into knots, I gave up. I needed to talk to someone about all this. A non-Dad, non-Ben someone.

I knew who that someone was.

And for the first time, I didn't need it to be El Cid.

Pulling on jeans and a shirt from the pile on the floor, I stuffed my feet into a pair of sneakers, grabbed my mace, and got to sneaking through the house. I eased open the screen, glad Dad had left the front door ajar for the night breeze, and edged out sideways.

"Is something wrong, *mijo?*"

I jumped at my father's voice. Half lit by the half moon, he was seated at the far end of the porch, slouched in a lawn chair and bare feet propped on the rail. His mace rested across his lap.

"I can't sleep." I joined him, leaning against the rail. "My head is too full."

"That is certainly a first." His smile was a flash of white in the darkness.

"Ha, ha." I pointed my chin at Dad's weapon. "On watch?"

"No, he is not." Turk's disembodied voice floated across the yard. "That's what he's got *me* for." I squinted toward the barn. A large black shape moved in the building's darker shadow.

"And I appreciate your vigilance, *mi amigo*," Dad called. "But I believe we are safe for now. Please rest."

"Rest is for slackers." Turk stomped once. Sparks burst from under his shoe. Equine fireworks. "I'll be in the east field if you need me. And Javier? What I said about the boys? Think about it, okay?"

"I will give it my deepest consideration."

Turk grumbled under his breath as he walked away. The crunch of hoof on gravel faded after a few minutes.

"What boys? Did he mean Ben and me?"

"Stubborn as an ox, although I would not dare say it to his face," Dad said, ignoring my question. "Our zealous friend is determined to guard our sleep tonight."

I nudged his leg with the butt-end of my mace. "You didn't answer me."

Dad sighed. "Turk is of the opinion that I should send you and Ben away until he and I have dealt with this *bruja*. He thinks you and your brother would be safer somewhere else, and that he would be better able to focus on keeping *me* alive and not you two as well."

"Turk the Jerk is *worried*? About *us*?" I snorted. "Yeah. Right."

"I wish you would not call him that. Even in jest. He *is* trying, my son."

I thought back to all the times Turk mashed our toes with his bucket-size hooves—accidentally, he would always claim, the big liar—or knocked us over or called us little rats. *Sure he is. Trying to make our lives miserable.*

Knowing Dad was caught between his war-brother and his sons, I decided to give him a break and took my turn at changing the subject. "Do you really think Hester Lemprey is going to give us three days?" I hopped up on the rail, managing to whack my shin with my mace. Wincing, I rubbed it as I waited for Dad's answer.

He scratched his goatee. "In a strange way, I do. A strategic error on her part as it gives us time to come up with our own plan." Rising, he stretched and yawned as he peered at the sky.

"Think I'll stay up a little longer. Maybe," I flapped a hand toward the barn, "hang out with Rigo."

Dad nodded. "A tried-and-true method of head-emptying." He glanced down at me. "Stay with the horses. You have your weapon? *Bueno.* Not too late, now." He disappeared inside.

Armed with my mace and my father's blessing, I headed across the yard. Halfway there, Rigo appeared in the barn's doorway. He stepped out.

I ran a hand down his neck. "Guess you heard me."

He chuffed. "We hear everything you guys say. Even when you're inside the house, especially if the front door or windows are open."

"Eavesdropping?" I teased.

Rigo twitched a shoulder. "More like early reconnaissance. We can protect you better when we know what's going on." He turned sideways. "Let's take a walk."

Resting my mace across his withers, I crouched slightly, then leaped as high as I could, landing stomach-down with a grunt. A few kicks with my legs, and kneeing him twice in the ribs, and I was mounted. "Sorry."

He sighed. "We have *got* to work on that."

Weapon across my lap, I rode holding on with nothing but balance and twelve years of practice under my belt. We walked around the south end of the barn and headed out to the field. Squinting, I could just make out Turk's silhouette at the far end, while out in the middle, Izzie grazed, her mane and tail pale blurs in the moonlight. In the quiet of the night, I caught the faint sound of her teeth ripping the grass.

I took a deep breath, then another. The air was a blend of the cool breeze off the mountains mixed with the dusty tang of sage and creosote and horse. Overhead the stars— so thick they were smudges of light instead of tiny dots— tried to outshine the half moon but failed. Looking down, I noticed Rigo and I cast a centaur's shadow.

Ambling, Rigo took a slow circuit around the field, his head bobbing. With every stride, I felt the knots inside of me loosen a little.

"One crazy horse of a day, no?" he said after a few minutes.

"That's an understatement."

He flicked an ear back. "What's bothering you the most? Hester Lemprey or the thought of stepping into your father's boots?"

"Both." I sighed.

"Well, you know we're not going to let some B-grade witch mess with the family. Sure, she's packing that wand, but there's only one of her and there's three of us. Plus three of you guys. Six to one makes for some solid odds."

"And Dad's got some ideas too. About defending ourselves." My earlier notion about the shield ghosted through my head. It vanished before I could grab it.

Rigo halted. "And taking over the ranch some day?"

I lowered myself backward and stretched out flat, my legs dangling on either side of Rigo's barrel, my head pillowed on his haunch, and my nose and chin pointed at the stars. "One minute, I can't stand the thought of Ben being gone or Dad not hunting anymore. Then the next minute, I can see myself doing it. Taking care of the place. Keeping the skinners in check. Helping the other Knights when they need me. Heck, if Dad could do all that by himself at nineteen, then I should be able to handle it when I'm older." I reached down and patted his side. "Especially since I've got you as a partner. You watch—we'll be the dream team everyone talks about."

Rigo chuffed softly, ribs rising and falling beneath me. "Appreciate the vote of confidence. Still…" He hesitated.

"What?"

"I'm not El Cid, you know."

Something in his voice made me sit up. Frowning, I threw a leg over his neck and slid to the ground and walked around until we were nose to nose. "What's going on? Did Turk say something? Look, just ignore the big burro."

He snorted, blowing my hair off my forehead. "Like I'd listen to him anyway. No, it's more that sometimes I feel the pressure."

I was pretty sure I knew what he was talking about. I asked anyway. "What pressure?"

"To perform. To live up to expectations. El Cid wasn't just any warhorse. He was… *El Cid*. He set some freaking high hurdles for the rest of us to jump. Big horseshoes to fill and all that. Know what I mean?"

"Are you kidding? *I'm* the youngest son of a legend, remember?"

"Yeah, well." He pawed at the grass. "I just don't want to let you down. Or Javier."

Something welled up in my chest and pushed against my eyeballs. I reached up and smoothed aside the hank of forelock that always flopped over one eye, just like my hair did when it got too long. I cleared my throat. "You know, Rigo. Dad said something to me the other day when he asked how you and I were getting along. Been thinking about it."

Rigo pricked his ears in question.

Hoping I'd get the right words in the right order, I spoke slowly. "He said that even through he and El Cid were a solid team, it hadn't happened overnight. That it took time. They had to hunt together for years and learn from each other along the way. Lots of near misses. Lots of wins, too." I peered into his eyes. "Does that make sense?"

Rigo butted his forehead against my chest, then left it there. "Okay, then. We'll take this one stride at a time."

I ran my hand along his neck, then buried my fingers in his mane. It felt all kinds of good to know he had my back. Still, a gnat-sized question—one that I had ignored ever since Rigo joined us—hummed through my skull. Why *had* Rigo decide to stay with us? I mentally swatted the question away. *What does it matter? He's here now and that's what counts.*

Still…

11

"**M**att? They are here."

At Dad's announcement, I hurried through the house, mace dangling from my wrist and whacking my leg every other stride. I was getting really, *really* sick of carrying it around. I stepped out onto the porch and joined my father.

Dr. Vandermer's dark green station wagon appeared around the Hump in a flurry of dust lit up by the mid-morning sun. Out of the corner of my eye, I noticed Dad whisking horsehair off the front of his fancy going-to-town white cowboy shirt. His own weapon hung from his wrist.

"Kind of dressed up just to drive to Denver."

My father shrugged. "Simply a clean shirt."

I glanced up at the black cowboy hat brushed free of dust, then down at the polished boots. "Sure, Dad. Whatever."

"Did you hang fresh towels in your bathroom?" Dad made a hard change to the subject. "Neatly?"

"For the third time, yes. And you know Perry—she doesn't care about stuff like that."

"Even so, she is our guest and I want her to feel welcome." As the Vandermer's Subaru rolled to a stop in a crunch of gravel, he removed his hat and walked down the steps.

Perry flung the door open, then scrambled out, dragging a day pack with her. She grinned, her dark eyes tipping at the corners. "Here. Catch." She tossed the pack to me, then opened the back door and hauled out a larger duffle with a grunt. "This one, I won't throw. Might hurt both of us." She dragged it up the steps before I could help her. Dropping the bag on the porch, she looked around. Her short black hair framed her face in wisps. "Where are Izzie and the guys?"

"Training run to the Maze and back," I said. "They go early before it gets too hot." I looked past her and smiled a hello at her mom stepping out of the car.

Dr. Vandermer slammed the door with a look of exasperation. Maybe because she was wearing a suit instead of her usual T-shirt and jeans and sneakers. A line between her blue eyes, she sighed, then blew a strand of blonde hair out of her face.

Perry complained more than once that it drove her insane when people would stare at her mother's pale coloring, then Perry's dark features, then ask the same awkward half-question: "Is your daughter...?"

"It's not that I mind people asking if I'm adopted, because I'm totally cool with it," Perry had explained, "and I would ask if I were them. No, it's the way Mom launches into this long story about how she flew to China to adopt me when I was a baby, and how she fell in love with me the first nano-second she saw me, and how I'm über-smart and talented and athletic, and *gaaah*, please just kill me now."

"I swear, the one morning I need to be on time, I end up running late." Dr. Vandermer stalked around the front of the car. "Listen, Jav, are you sure about taking me up there? I don't mind parking at the airport that long. The Museum is footing the bill. This is your last chance to get out of a long drive back from Denver."

"I am happy to do so," Dad said. "But I, too, will ask again. Are *you* certain about Perry staying here? This Hester Lemprey. I do not know how dangerous things might become."

"Whoa. Stop right there." She held up a hand. "I told you last night when you called, if you and your sons can't keep my daughter safe, no matter what the danger is, then who can?"

"Fighting a sorceress is not like hunting skinners."

"I know, Jav," Dr. Vandermer said. "But this is our new reality. Mine and Perry's. A reality that includes talking horses and skinners and witches and goblins and who knows what else. Perry's been hoping for dragons, but I told her the closest she'd ever get to a dragon was that fossilized ancestor of velociraptor scientists discovered in northeast China a few years ago." She grinned. "You hunters makes paleontology seem about as exciting as taking out the garbage."

Dad shook his head. "You are remarkable, Liz."

"That I am." She nodded in agreement. "You're not too bad yourself."

They smiled at each other long enough to be weird.

"Make them stop," Perry whispered.

"Wish I could," I muttered back.

"Perry." Dr. Vandermer motioned her over. "Be helpful. Mind Mr. Del Toro."

"I know how to behave." Perry returned her mom's hug, then wiggled free.

"Bye, Matt. Thanks for sharing your room with Ben." Dr. Vandermer smiled at me, then slid behind the wheel and started the car.

Dad opened the passenger door. "I will be home by supper. Rigo and Isabel said if they were not too tired when they returned, they would take you and Perry for a ride. I told them to stay on the road." He climbed in. *Take your weapon*, he signaled through the window.

I nodded. Perry and I waved from the porch until the car disappeared around the Hump.

"Okay, I want to hear all about the witch." Perry grabbed her duffel, staggering a step.

"Trade you." Handing her the day pack, I hoisted up the larger bag, then led the way to Ben's room and dropped it in the middle of the floor. "Sorry you're stuck in here."

"Sorry you have to share your room with him."

I shrugged. "Mine has twin beds. And it's just for ten days." Now that I knew Ben might be leaving sooner than later, sharing a room with him didn't seem all that bad. Okay, maybe just a little bit.

She tossed her pack on the bed. "Where *is* Ben, anyway?"

"Town. He and a friend are working on our truck." I gestured at the dresser. "Bottom two drawers are yours if you want them."

"I'm cool with living out of my bag. Nothing in there but jeans and shorts and T-shirts. Oh, and one skirt. Because you never know, young lady," her voice shifted into an imitation of her mother's, "when you might go somewhere nice. Sheesh, that's what clean jeans are for. And these." Beaming, she stuck a foot out. "Finally got boots. Ropers. Just like yours. 'Course I owe Mom about seven years of indentured servitude to pay for them." She blew her bangs out of her eyes. "Speaking of Mom."

"What about her?"

"She pretends she isn't, but she *is* a little worried."

"I don't blame her," I said. "First skinners, then a sorceress. Pretty crazy."

"Exactly. So. Just to help *her* feel less nervous about stuff, I was wondering..." She pointed at my mace.

"If you're going to ask me again to teach you how to use it, the answer is still no. Dad said he'd kill me if I ever let you get that close to something that needed smashed and dashed. Sorry."

"No, you're not. But I get it. I'm not going to give up asking. Who knows, someday maybe you'll need *me* to save *your* ham hock." With a double forehand, she swung an imaginary mace through the air, then held it aloft. "VANDERMER!"

"Seriously? You want to go with *Vandermer* as your war cry?"

"Why not? You guys have Santiago as yours. Why can't I use Vandermer?"

"Santiago sounds cool. Vandermer just sounds like a type of Dutch cookie."

A faint popcorn crunch of hooves on gravel was followed by Izzie calling Perry's name.

"Move, move!" Perry pushed around me, darted down the hall, and out the front door. I followed, catching the screen before it slapped me in the face.

Perry missed the first step, stumbled on the second step, but caught herself by the third and hit the ground with a grunt. "Izzie!" She sprinted across the yard, boots slipping, and flung her arms around the sorrel's sweat-streaked neck.

The warhorse nuzzled her. "Sorry about the gross. Hard workout."

Perry blew a raspberry. "Like I care."

She followed Izzie over the water barrel. The mare plunged her nose in, sloshed it around a few times, then began slurping. Her ears waggled back and forth as Perry asked about the unfinished patch job on the barn, one hand buried in the sorrel's mane.

I walked over to Rigo. He stood with head lowered and ribs rising and falling. Foam flecked his neck and chest and even the corners of his mouth. Against his brown coat, it looked like whipped cream on chocolate. Stretching out my T-shirt, I wiped his face dry. Two seconds later, I remembered it was one of my good shirts. *Well, not anymore.*

"You okay?" I pushed his forelock to one side.

"Izzie may be slower than me in a sprint," he panted, "but dang. She's got endurance with a capital I."

"Capital *e*, you mean. Endurance starts with an e, not an i."

"Whatever it starts with, she finished it. She even made Turk suffer for it this time."

Speak of the devil. I glanced down the drive. "Where *is* he, anyway?"

Izzie swung her head around, dripping water on Perry. "Good question."

"When did you see him last, Iz?" A tiny worry worm squirmed up my neck and into my hair.

"By the Gate. We took a break in the shade for a few minutes, then headed home. Turk stopped to give some grief to a rattlesnake that wouldn't yield the trail."

"Or introduce himself as a long-lost cousin," Rigo said. "We didn't want to interrupt a family reunion, so Iz and I went on ahead."

"Still." Izzie flicked her ears. "He shouldn't be *this* far behind us." She wheeled about and jogged down the drive. Reaching the spot where it curved around the Hump, she paused, head raised high. I could see her tail slashing back and forth, like a cat stalking a birdfeeder.

"Any sign?" I hollered.

Glancing over her shoulder, she shook her head. "Want me to go look for him?" she called.

Stay together, boys. I heard El Cid's voice in my head, admonishing me and Ben every time we took off to play. *If something happens, don't split up. Wait, and either your father or I will come.* I waved at her to come back.

"So, what's the plan?" she asked, trotting up.

I didn't like the way they all stared at me like I had one. How was I supposed to know what to do?

"I'll call Ben." I reached into my back pocket and pulled out my cell. The call went right to voice mail. Guess he was head-down in the truck's engine. I waited for the beep, then spoke. "Hey. Turk never came back from the morning workout. Izzie and Rigo did and they're fine." I hesitated. "We're going to go look for him." I set the volume to max, then put it away.

"Why?" Rigo curled his lip. "The jerk can take care of himself."

"Because..." I flapped a hand around. "Because he's *our* jerk."

"Javier will come unglued on us warhorses if he hears we took you two out there," Rigo said. "Especially with that *bruja* and her crystal cracker prowling around."

Izzie snorted. "Staying *here* isn't any safer. Hester Lemprey could've fried us yesterday, but like she said, she's got standards. No, I think it's cool for a few more days."

"And Mr. Del Toro said we could take a ride if you guys weren't too tired," Perry added.

"On the *road*," Rigo pointed out. "Not to the Maze."

"Not to insult you," Izzie sniffed, "but are you channeling El Cid or something? What's with the overly protective jam?"

Rigo's nostrils flared. "In case you've forgotten, it's our *job* to keep our partners *safe*."

The sorrel tossed her head. "*And* to help them deal with whatever creepy creature shows up. We're *warhorses*, not nanny goats. Right, Matt?"

I didn't answer. Instead, I thought about last night. Was I really going to be the one running the ranch? Taking the lead on hunts? Deciding when and how much to risk?

I took a deep breath. "We're going after Turk. Yeah, I know it might be risky, but we need to check that he's okay."

As Perry and I hurried to the barn to saddle up Izzie and Rigo, I hoped I hadn't just made the worst decision in the entire history of the known universe.

12

"Hey, Perry?" Hands on autopilot, I fastened Rigo's halter, then looked across the barn and braced myself to face the battle. "Maybe you should stay here. Izzie'll keep you company. Rigo and I can handle this."

With a grunt, Perry hoisted the saddle up onto Izzie's back. "Did you hear Matt suggest we hang back?"

"If he did," the warhorse shook the saddle into place with a jingle of buckles, "*I* didn't catch it."

I groaned. "C'mon, Perry. Help me out here."

"We are. That's why we're coming, too." Perry fished the cinch around the sorrel's belly and secured the buckle. "How's that?"

Izzie took a breath and let it out. "Tighter, please."

I tried again. "Perry, you don't understand—"

"I do, Matt. You've trained your whole life for this kind of stuff, and I haven't, and you don't want anything to happen to me because I'm your friend." She gave the strap a final tug. "Well, guess what. I don't want anything to happen to *you*, either. Or Rigo."

"And there's no way I'm letting you guys ride out there alone," Izzie added. "This conversation is done and dusted. Time to roll, girlfriend."

Perry squirrel-climbed into the saddle and wiggled her right foot around until she found the stirrup, then gathered up the reins. "Okay, all set. Let's go find our lost sheep."

"*Black* sheep." Izzie chuffed. She trotted out of the barn, Perry pointedly ignoring me.

"Dude." Fuming, I turned on Rigo. "Why didn't you say anything? Back me up?"

"Because I agree with her. No, *not* about bringing Perry along—that's stupid, and a total Izzie move—but about her coming with us. If there's trouble, I'd just as soon have Izzie beside us. She's good. Like really good."

Always listen to the warhorses. That was one of our family's top three rules. The other rules were do not get dead and do not get your brother dead.

"Fine. Whatever. Nobody listen to me." I swung up on my war-brother's back. Now I knew how Dad felt when everyone argued with him.

Leaving the cool of the barn, the sun's heat slapped me in the face and pressed down on the top of my head. Breaking into a trot, Rigo caught up with Izzie and Perry. Side by side, the horses jogged along the road, accompanied by the familiar theme song of creaking leather, ringing buckles, and the dull thud of hoof on earth. Dust rose, the grains as fine as cinnamon. A lazy breeze started up, rolling from the mountains and across the prairie; the tall grasses bowed to us as we passed.

"Glad we're going after Turk," Perry said. Moving in time with Izzie's light-as-a-feather gait, she untangled strands of mane from the reins. "I know he's a real piece of work, *and* a bully, but…"

I waited. "But what?"

"Don't laugh, okay?" She smoothed the hairs in place. "Sometimes, I feel sorry for him. Always being the outsider. Especially in this family. You guys are all pretty tight."

Rigo snorted. "His choice, not ours."

"Hey, I tried early on." Izzie pointed an ear back at us. "But he was such a donkey to Ben that I gave up. Except for Javier, Turk won't let anyone get close."

Perry shrugged. "Maybe he doesn't know how."

I didn't say anything. Hard to talk when truth pokes a cold finger in one's gut.

We rode in silence for the next mile and a half. Ahead of us, a lonely sign waited by the side of the road. Reaching it, we paused. Beyond the sign, the dirt road arrowed north toward the looming mesa. Weeds grew along its center strip in a Mohawk haircut.

I eyed the wooden board. Even with the dust and rain and wind and one heck of a hailstorm last week, the words were still readable: *El Laberinto Research Project in Session. Approved Visitors Only. Thank you for your cooperation. The Field Museum, Chicago.* The institute's logo—an image of a Greek-like temple—decorated a lower corner.

Rising in the stirrups, I held the horn for balance and squinted around. Head lifted, Rigo swiveled his ears this way and that. Izzie aimed her nose upward, nostrils working as she read the wind.

"Well?" Even as I asked, I knew the answer. An enormous black stallion would be hard to miss on that much lonesome prairie.

The sorrel shook her head. "Just a whole lot of open range."

Perry gestured toward the Maze. "Would he have gone inside?"

I studied the orphaned mesa. Even with the August sun doing a number on me, cold dread ran down my spine. "Why would he?"

"Maybe to check on the coffers?" Rigo shifted from leg to leg. "You know, to make sure Hester Lemprey hadn't messed with them. Except he's too big to get inside the cave."

"But he *could* tell if anyone or anything has been near it." Perry pushed her sweaty bangs off her forehead. They poked straight up. "Skinners leave tracks. Wouldn't Hester Lemprey leave tracks, too?"

"Unless she's riding a broom," Izzie said.

"Dad thinks she can't get past the wards for that very reason," I said. "Because she *is* a sorceress."

"He *thinks*." Perry raised her eyebrows. "But he doesn't *know* for sure."

I shrugged. "He said we won't really know until she actually tries. But I'm with Rigo—Turk probably went in." *And he should've been out by now.* I touched Rigo's side with a heel.

He took two running steps, then broke into a lope. With every stride, the gap in the wall grew larger and larger, like a giant ogre's mouth. *Open wide, here comes some fresh children.* I twisted the mace's leather throng more tightly around my wrist and rested the weapon on my right thigh.

A few yards from the Gate, the horses dropped to a walk, then halted. The foot of the wall was littered with massive boulders and smaller rubble the mesa had shed over thousands upon thousands of years. Geological dandruff. I looked up.

So did Perry. "I've always wondered," she eyed the tops of the buttes, "how *did* Santiago get the wards up there?"

"Nobody knows."

"What do they look like? The wards. How do they work?"

I thought for a moment, trying to remember Dad's description. "They're round and flat. This big, I think." I held my hands about a foot apart. "They're made out of iron and they've got our family sigil on one side. Dad and Roman both think that the same magic that powers our maces and the coffers also powers the wards. He said the magic originated from the royal blessing that the queen of Spain gave Santiago and the other Knights right before they sailed to the New World."

"And that blessing is still working?" Perry asked, her chin aimed skyward. "Even after four centuries?"

"Guess there's not an expiration date on magical mojo." I yanked my attention from the towers and eyed the Gate.

The opening was a dark corridor leading to nowhere a sane person would ever want to go. Cool air flowed out. I plucked at my shirt, letting the breeze dry my sweat. Perry chewed on her lip, a line between her brows.

"Well?" Izzie stomped a hoof. "What are we waiting for?"

"One does not simply walk into the Maze," Perry murmured. One hand gripped the reins, the knuckles white. Guess she was remembering the last time she was in there.

Rigo tensed, then flung up his head, almost whacking me in the face with the back of his skull. Next to us, Izzie stood her ground, ears pricked and tail whipping her hindquarters. Perry wrapped a hand around the saddle horn.

"What is it, Rigo? Skinners?" I stared into the darkness, my pulse a *whomp, whomp, whomp* in my ears. My head knew they couldn't get past the wards. The rest of me wasn't so sure. I squeezed the mace's haft.

Then, both horses relaxed. They glanced at each other and nodded.

"Everyone can stand down," Rigo said. "It's not a skinner."

Izzie chuffed. "Smells about as bad, though."

A blurry shape moved in the darkness. The clink of metal on rock. The blur grew bigger and bigger, and then stepped out of the shadows.

"Turk." Perry blew out a long breath. "Whew. Glad you're okay."

"Why wouldn't I be okay?" He glared at us. "Now, before I kick you oxheads all the way back to the ranch, tell me what you were thinking coming out here? Oh. Wait." He sneered. "Matt's here. So, forget about any kind of thinking."

"What's going on?" Distrust fluttered around inside my head. "What were you doing in there?"

"Rock climbing." The black stallion shouldered between Rigo and Izzie. Raising his tail, he farted.

I fanned a hand in front of my nose. "You're hiding something."

"Or he *did* something," Rigo flattened his ears, "that he doesn't want anyone to know about."

Izzie nodded. "That's why he snuck off behind our backs. To cover it up or—"

"Has it occurred to you jack-a-dopes," Turk paused, then turned around, "that I might be doing something on Javier's request?"

Never crossed my mind. I blinked. "Um…"

"Didn't think so." He nodded toward the ranch. "Move your hindquarters. I'll be right on your heels."

Rigo stiffened. "We don't take orders from you."

Izzie curled her lip. "Heck, we barely take *notice* of you."

"Well, take notice of *this*." Turk crowded Izzie. "With El Cid dead and Javier away, *I'm* boss hoss around here, sweetheart."

Izzie crowded right back. "In your dreams. If anyone's in charge right now, it's Ben."

"*Ben?*" Rigo snorted. "Yeah, I don't think so. Look, Izzie, I get that he's your hunting partner, but c'mon. We all know he's not going to stick around. So, if anyone is the new sheriff in town, it's Matt."

Everyone looked at me; I was really starting to not like that. Was I supposed to say something? Act like I knew what I was doing? I felt like a fake because I didn't have a clue.

Turk huffed. "Kidding, right? Heck, you might as well put *Perry* in charge."

Perry narrowed her eyes. "And here I was feeling sorry for you, Turk. Guess that was a waste of brain space."

"See, *that's* the problem with talking horses." From behind a nearby boulder the size of a compact car, a tall figure stepped out. "They've got an opinion about every-thing and they never shut up."

Rigo and Izzie whirled on their hind legs; only a death grip on the horn kept Perry from flying out of the saddle. Turk shoved between the other warhorses and took up a position in front. Tightening my grip on my mace, I signaled Rigo with my legs and urged him forward.

In spite of the heat, Hester Lemprey wore the same leather jacket. Maybe she was like a rattlesnake and needed the warmth to stay alive.

Izzie stomped a hoof. "How'd she sneak up on *us*?" I could tell she was royally irked that something had gotten past their ears and noses.

"Doesn't matter." Turk started toward her. "She's finished."

"No, Turk," I hissed. The memory of those fireballs raced through my head.

Hester Lemprey raised a hand. "Whoa there, big guy." Reaching inside her jacket, she pulled out the wand. The crystal pulsed with a sickly yellow glow. She pointed it at

Turk. "Keep your distance or I'll blast your legs off. See how you like scooting around on your belly."

Turk flattened his ears. "Charming."

"Izzie." My eyes on the sorceress, I spoke out of the corner of my mouth. "Take Perry and get out of here."

"No way," they both said at the same time.

I ground my teeth. Ignoring Hester Lemprey's smirk, I raised my chin. "What are you doing here?"

"Oh, just prowling. But, hey, since you're not doing anything, how about you save us all some time and go get the chest. As I said yesterday, I'll pay a fair price, then be out of your lives. It'll be like I was never here."

Suspicion poked me in the back. "What's the deal with you and that coffer?" *And why don't you just go get it yourself? It is because you can't?*

"I just want to make good on a promise. One that has nothing to do with you Knights. And, yeah, I'll bet your daddy—who, by the way, is one cool drink of sangria and you can tell him I said that—claims that once I get my hands on *El Cofre Rojo*," she pronounced the name with a flare, "I'll let loose all seven levels of Dante's Inferno. Well, that's not true. Whatever was in that chest is now just dust and bones."

No matter if she really believed that or was just slinging baloney, I knew it wasn't true. I wondered if there was a way I could trick her into revealing why she *really* wanted it. Even better, if she could actually get past the wards. *Know your enemy.* One of Dad's favorite maxims whispered in my head. "You sure about that? That what's inside is really dead?"

Hester Lemprey froze at my words. She licked her lips. "Wait. You opened it?" Her eyes narrowed into chips of blue ice. "What did you see?"

Faking indifference, I thought about that reptilian hand finger-walking its way out of the chest right before I sealed it. "Gee, that was a super busy day. Hard to remember all the details."

"Better figure out a way." She pointed the crystal at my head. "*Now.*"

Rigo tensed. So did I. Izzie backed up a step, in spite of Perry's protest. Turk rumbled a warning.

"I *said*." Red splotches flared on the sorceress's cheeks. "What was inside? Was it alive?"

Suspicion went from poking me to punching me between the shoulder blades. "Maybe. Maybe not."

She eyed me for a minute, mouth working, then she relaxed and lowered the crystal. "Nice try." She sneered. "But I can tell you're lying."

I shrugged. "Well, whatever it was, I'm guessing it was something bad. Something *evil*. Why else would it have been locked up?"

"News flash, kid. In this day and age, evil is relative." Lips pursed, she glanced at the Gate again and then back at me. "So, Ben, right?"

"Matt."

"Matt. Sure you don't want to take a little ride and get it for me? Like I said yesterday, it's a straightforward business transaction. Oodles of cash in the deal. I'm thinking thirty thousand's a fair price. And there'll be one less creepy casket to watch over. Everyone will be snap-happy."

"Something to consider," Rigo muttered.

I ignored him. "Wouldn't do you any good even if we did hand it over. The coffer's sealed shut." *So there.*

"Not a problem. I've got some tricks." She waggled her crystal.

Dang it.

"You want it so bad, why don't *you* go inside and get it?" I said. "Or is something stopping you?" I held my breath.

Hester Lemprey tightened her jaw. Her face, already splotchy, grew redder until I swore she was going to burst into flame. My heart leaped. *That's it! She can't get past the wards!*

"What's stopping me," she ground out between her teeth, "is that I promised I'd give you three days. And my word is good. That said, one day is half over. You got two left. Make the right decision." Her eyes flickered over to Perry. "Before someone gets hurt."

Izzie bared her teeth. "Go ahead. Threaten Perry again. Give me an excuse."

The sorceress backed up, crystal leveled at the sorrel. "Love your moxie, girlfriend, but dial it down." Taking another step, she stumbled over a rock, then caught herself. "Tell Javier I'll meet him right here in two days. Let's make it high noon. You know, for that whole cowboy vibe. Oh, and just in case." She pulled something from an inside pocket and held it up. "My business card. I'm staying in town at the Best Western, which, by the way, is neither. Call me if you change your mind." She dropped it. Letting it flutter to the ground, she disappeared around the boulder. A few moments later, I heard a motorcycle engine cough once then kick to life. With a roar, she burst into view, crouched forward over the handlebars. In a spray of dirt and grass and rocks, she sped away, bouncing and careening across the prairie toward the road.

Letting out a long breath, I relaxed my fingers, then scrubbed my sticky palm along my jeans. "Guess Dad was right. She can't get past the wards." Swinging out of the saddle, I dropped to the ground, knees wobbling.

"And she's clueless about what's really inside," Rigo added. "Whoa there." He planted his chin on my shoulder as I started forward. "Where're you going?"

"To get her card." I slipped free and hurried over and snatched it up. Walking back, I studied it. Printed on thick white stock, the block letters spelled out her name and a cell phone number with an area code I didn't recognize. That was all. I shoved it in my back pocket and remounted.

My own phone blared just as my rump touched leather. I jumped. So did everyone else. I pulled it out and tapped on the screen, putting it on speaker. "Hey."

"I'm on my way." Ben's voice faded in and out. "Where are you? Did Turk show up?"

"Yeah, he's fine. Listen, we just ran into Hester Lemprey and I don't think she can get inside—"

"SHE'S *THERE*? AT THE *RANCH*?" Over my brother's bellow, I caught the familiar rattle as the truck raced along the dirt road. He must have goosed the engine, because the grumble became a shriek.

"No, we're at the Gate. But she's gone. Nothing happened. Everything's cool. It's all good. In fact, I just figured out—"

"Who's *we*?" Ben shouted. "Tell me Perry's not with you."

She crowded closer, her knee digging into my leg. "I'm right here. Got a problem with that?"

Ben groaned. "How could you be so stupid, Matt? You know Dad will end us if anything happens to her."

Perry snatched the phone from me. "Just so you know," she yelled into the device, "I make my own decisions, and in this case, I decided to come along and see if I could help find Turk. Not like *you* were around. Oh, and by the way, stop talking about me like I'm some kind of... of... *damsel*."

I bit down on a laugh. Turk chuffed. Rigo did too, then turned it into a cough when Izzie narrowed her eyes. With a glare that matched the sorrel's, Perry threw the phone at me.

I almost fumbled the catch. Snagging it with both hands, I hugged it to my chest. "We're heading home now." I hit the end button and shoved the phone in my back pocket.

Turk stuck his nose close to Perry's ear. "Let me know," he said in a low tone, "if you want me to give Ben an attitude adjustment when the ginger's not around."

"Don't tempt me." Perry glowered.

"I can hear you guys, you know," Izzie said, ears flat along her skull.

By the time we got back, Ben was in the yard. He waited by the truck, fists on his hips and a scowl on his face.

"Does Ben know how much he looks like Javier when he does that?" Rigo asked.

"Nope," I said. "You want to tell him?"

"Nah, I'm good."

We rode closer. Turk made a beeline for the water barrel and began slurping. With a word to Perry, Izzie carried her inside the barn and disappeared. I slid from Rigo's back.

Ben shook his head. "You are so dead. When Dad finds out what went down today, he'll—"

"*If* he finds out."

"Oh, he'll find out. Turk'll spill it as soon as Dad gets home. Just to get us in trouble."

We both sighed. Then Ben added, "And then Pop'll blame me."

"Why? He knew you were in town. And anyway, it was *my* call, not yours." After the whole-taking-over-the-family-business business, my decisions seemed to weigh me down like walking around with boots full of water. Was this what life was going to be like when I was in charge?

"We'll see." He hoisted himself up on the wall of the truck bed. "So, what were you going to tell me about Hester Lemprey? You must've chapped her something fierce because she about ran me off the road."

I told Ben about what Dad and I had theorized, and how Hester Lemprey tried to get me to go inside the Maze for the casket. "Being a sorceress, she can't get past the wards. She needs *us* to get inside. For once," I spun my mace into the air, then caught it by the haft, "*we've* got the upper hand over the bad guys."

"Think again, little brother."

My grin slipped a notch. "What do you mean?"

"She only needs *one* of us to ride into the Maze and fetch it. What's stopping her from blasting us or the horses or Perry—one by one—until we perform?"

He was talking about hostages. My heart plummeted to sea level. "I never thought of that."

"But, hey. Look on the bright side. That's a whole two days away. Right now, you've got something worse to worry about."

"What?"

He jumped down and cuffed me on the head. "How to explain to Dad why you took Perry to the Maze."

14

"Not to keep saying it." Perry opened one kitchen drawer, then another, rattling utensils around. She pulled out a handful of spoons and waggled them at me. "But you really should tell your father before Turk does."

"Then stop saying it." I lifted the lid on the slow cooker and sampled the stew that had simmered all day. The aroma of beef and onions and Worcestershire sauce filled the kitchen, along with the corn muffins Ben had figured out how to make from a mix. He even put together a salad, complete with tomatoes and cucumbers and avocadoes. Wonders never ceased.

All three of us were banging into each other in the small kitchen, scrambling to have supper ready and waiting. Ben and I knew from experience that a hungry Dad was a low and mean creature. Didn't want to give him any more ammo.

Stirring the stew, I tensed at the hum of an approaching car. Perry and I looked at each other.

"Sounds like Mom's." She rubbed her hands together. "I'm kind of nervous. Is he a yeller or does he go for the guilt lecture?"

"Oh, you're safe." I kept one eye on the front screen. "He won't get mad at you. You're our guest."

"And a girl." Ben said. "Dad is crazy about you because he and Mom always wanted a daughter." At my gasp of astonishment, he continued. "Yeah, El Cid told me once that Mom and Dad were planning on another baby right before she died. Trying for a girl."

"Whoa. I would've been the middle kid instead of the youngest." For a moment, I tried to imagine our family whole again. With Mom. And maybe another sibling.

The slam of a car door. *Might as well get this over with*. I trudged out of the kitchen and slipped through the screen door and waited on the porch. "Supper's ready."

Walking around the front of the station wagon, Dad smiled. "See, this is why I wanted children. Ready-made servants." Hat in hand and mace on wrist, he climbed the steps, then paused, rolling his head from side to side. "Everything is okay? I saw Rigo and Isabel in the field as I drove past, but no Turk."

"Oh, he's around. Probably in the barn." I swallowed. "I, um, I need to tell you something before..." My words fled at the appearance of the black stallion strolling out of the building. Great. Just great.

"One moment, Matt." Dad turned. "Turk? Any sign?"

"All clear, Javier." He paused at the lowest step and stood eye to eye with us. "Of course, I couldn't get inside the cave, but there weren't any paw prints or footprints around the opening, except ours."

"*Gracias*, my friend."

Turk nodded once. "But I think Matt has something else to add. About the Maze." If horses could smirk, he would have. Jerk.

"I want to talk to my dad." I waited a beat. "*Alone*."

Turk glanced at Dad. My father waved him away.

I waited until the stallion disappeared around the far side of the barn, then took a deep breath, tightened the cinch around my courage, and busted out of the chute. "I rode to the Maze with Perry because Turk hadn't come back with Rigo and Izzie."

Dad stiffened. "You... you did *what?*"

"And no big deal, but we ran into Hester Lemprey near the Gate and guess what?" I plunged ahead before he could speak. "We found out she can't get inside the Maze because of the wards."

"*Madre de Dios*," Dad breathed. "The *bruja* was there?"

"Well, yeah. And, by the way, it wasn't Ben's fault because he didn't know, so don't get mad at him, okay? Oh, and did I mention the fact that you were right, and she can't get past the wards?" Out of words, I held my breath and waited, pulse whomping away.

Staring at me, Dad's face did that mask thing where I couldn't tell what he was thinking. Probably he was planning how to end me for putting Perry in danger. With a sigh, he raked his fingers through his hair, making it stick up on one side. "I am guessing Perry refused to stay behind. And Isabel backed her up?"

"Well..." Outside of Turk, nobody in our family snitched on each other. At least, not very much. Not if we could help it.

"Of course she did." He shook his head, jaw muscles jumping. "I will speak with them, especially our fine mare. She knows better."

I decided mentioning Rigo's defection wasn't worth, well, *mentioning*. "Cool, huh? About the wards and Hester Lemprey?"

"I had hoped it was true, but yes, it is good to have our theory confirmed." He shooed me inside. "Tell me everything over supper. And Matt?"

I paused, one hand on the screen handle. "Yeah?"

"Do *not* endanger Perry like that again. Because next time..." He nailed me with what Ben and I always called The Look of Impending Death.

I gulped and nodded.

❧

Once we were seated around the table, Dad made sure Perry was served first, then we all dug into our bowls. Between bites of painfully hot stew, I filled in the details. "She said to meet her there in two days at noon—except she called it *high* noon, for some reason. Did I leave anything out, Perry?"

"Not really." Perry blew on her spoonful. "But, wow, was she steamed she couldn't get inside the Maze. I thought she was going to blast holes in us like she did your barn." She slathered butter on her corn muffin and bit off the top. "I wonder if you could stick your own arm through your torso afterwards," she mused around a mouthful.

Ben made a face. "You're a sick puppy, Vandermer."

Chewing, she grinned.

Leaning back, Dad pushed his bowl aside and patted the corners of his mouth with a napkin. "On my way home, I spoke with Victoria Montoya. She confirmed what I had hoped. Our maces *will* destroy a sorceress just as they destroy skinners. A solid blow should do the trick."

Perry started to take another bite, then paused. "Destroy. As in... *kill* her?"

Dad shook his head. "I will not take her life unless forced to—not if there is any humanity left inside her. No, my goal is to destroy her wand. According to Victoria, a sorceress's power resides in her crystal. To use an archaic expression, she is wedded to the wand. Destroy it, and she will be harmless until she can craft another such weapon."

"Just one problem." Ben took another muffin and crumbled it into his stew. "Those fire bolts of hers. You're good with a mace, Dad, but not quick enough to deflect every one of Hester the Pester's fast balls."

"I will figure something out," Dad said. "I need only one strike."

"She only needs one, too," I said. "I don't see how you're going to get close enough to her wand without getting blasted..." I stopped, mouth open. Why hadn't I thought of this earlier?

"The shield!"

Everyone jumped at my shout. Perry choked, coughing and spewing out bits of muffin.

"What shield?" Ben asked, thumping her on the back.

"*Our* shield." I gestured toward the living room. "Santiago's shield. We could hold it up somehow so she can't hit us with her fireballs."

Ben snorted. "Besides the fact that none of us have ever trained with a shield and mace combo, what's stopping her from destroying *it*?"

"Oh." I slumped in my chair, cheeks growing hot. Duh.

"Actually, my son." Dad ran a thumb along his jaw as he studied me. "That is not a bad strategy. In fact, it is quite clever. The shield of Santiago is no less powerful than our maces or the wards. It carries not only our sigil, but also the royal blessing. It will defend me, especially if I use the remaining time to practice. Excuse me." He rose and carried his dishes to the sink and turned on the faucet.

It will defend *me*? I didn't like the sound of that. "You act like you're the only one who's going to fight her. What about Ben and me?"

"You two," he said over the whoosh of running water, "along with Perry and the horses, are to stay inside the Maze and behind the wards while I deal with that *bruja*. I am confident it will not take long."

"But—" I began.

"This is not a debate, Matt." Drying his hands, he turned around, then tossed the towel on the counter. "This is how it will be." He walked out the kitchen.

I stared after him. *No, Dad, it won't. Not if I can help it.*

"Matt. Wake up."

Some idiot with a death wish jabbed me. Hard. They kept at it until I pulled my face from the pillow. The room was filled with the soft blue-sage light of dawn. I blinked and looked up.

Ben loomed over me.

Right away, I knew something bad had happened. In my entire life, my brother had never, ever been awake before me.

I sat up, already fumbling for my mace on the floor by my bed. "What's going on?"

"Jo just called. Dad's talking to her right now. Something's wrong or she wouldn't have phoned him this early." He yanked on his jeans and shirt.

I pulled on the same clothes from yesterday and stumbled down the hall to our father's bedroom. Ben sank down on the foot of the bed. Already dressed in T-shirt, shorts, and running shoes for his daily lope to town and back, Dad held a finger to his lips as I appeared, then nodded at his cell phone laying on the nightstand.

"It's crazy right now, Javier." Josefina Navarre's voice rose from the speaker. "Dad and I thought we had thinned out the *duende* before he and Mom left. But, all of a sudden, I keep spotting one beastie after another. Vasco and I spent most of yesterday scouting the area and taking out those we could find. And the big lug won't admit it, but I think he might've strained a tendon in his right rear leg. He tried to pass it off like there was something in his shoe. We'll see." The sound of running water, then the gurgle of a coffee maker brewing away. "Is there anyway you and Turk could come down and help us out for a few days? I hate bothering you, but I don't want Mom and Dad coming home to a horde of *duendes* stinking up the ranch."

"You did the right thing to call me, Josefina." Rubbing the back of his neck, he studied me, then Ben, brows knitted together. I knew he was thinking about Hester Lemprey. "We have a small problem here, but I will find a way to arrive by noon—"

"Dad." Ben waved a hand and cut him off. "No, you stay here. *I'll* go. Better use of resources."

Our father thought for a moment. "Josefina? I will call you right back." He tapped on the screen. "What are you saying, Ben?"

"Jo just needs a second team to help out. And Izzie and I can hunt *duendes* in our sleep."

"What about Hester Lemprey?" I asked. *What if something goes wrong? What if we need you here?*

"If Dad can't handle her, nobody can. The timing stinks, but you know Jo wouldn't have called unless she really needed us. Well, one of us."

Staring into space, our father tugged at his goatee. "Leave Isabel here, Ben. You will make better time without the trailer."

My brother nodded. "Izzie will pitch a holy cow, but she'll understand. Hope so, anyway."

"How are you going to hunt without a warhorse?" I asked.

Ben shrugged. "Guess I'll team up with the Morrigan. That is, if she's feeling okay since losing the foal. And if she'll let me; she might want Jo instead. Although, to be honest, she's not as bad as Turk once you demonstrate you know which end of a mace to use."

I made a face. "That's not saying much." The Morrigan was Turk's dam. Not only did Turk inherit his mother's aggressive personality and fighting savvy, he also inherited the black mare's temperament—she wasn't named after the Celtic goddess of battle and death for nothing. The birth of her stillborn foal earlier in the summer hadn't improved her disposition, either.

Ben rose and headed for the door, then paused, one hand on the frame. "Just thought of something—if I take the truck, you guys are stranded out here without a vehicle."

"They can use my mom's car." Perry appeared in the doorway.

"Eavesdropping, *chica*?" A corner of Dad's mouth twitched.

She nodded. "One of my many superpowers. What's a den-day?"

"Dew-en-day." I corrected her. "A kind of goblin. Not as dangerous as skinners, but they stink like you don't want to know when whacked."

"Why do all the things you guys hunt have to smell bad?" Dressed in plaid pajama pants and a baggy T-shirt sporting a map of Middle-earth, Perry ducked under Ben's arm and joined us. "Anything I can do to help?"

"*Sí*, there is." Dad picked up the phone. "How good are you at throwing?"

Perry blinked. "You mean like throwing a... a *rock*?"

"I was thinking more a baseball."

I grinned. I knew what he was planning. "Good idea."

"Well," she said slowly. "I *was* on the sixth grade softball team last year at my old school. I played shortstop and was the backup pitcher. Why?"

"Batting practice," I said.

❦❧

Nothing made the hours fly like knowing a crazy sorceress was going to show up the next day, ready to rumble. By the time Ben had packed and left, Perry and I had taken care of horse chores, and Dad had returned from his run, it was already mid-morning before we headed out to the open field east of the barn.

Dad handled our maces and a couple of water bottles. I hauled a bucket filled with everything Perry and I could find to throw. A couple of baseballs. One softball. A can of tennis balls. And even some fist-sized rocks. A ball cap pulled low over her eyes, Perry insisted on carrying the shield, both arms stuck through the padded leather grips on its back. The horses ambled behind us.

"Is it heavy?" I asked Perry as we walked across the field. The grasses swayed in the ever-constant breeze flowing down from the mountains. Good thing, because my shirt was already sticking to me.

"Not too bad," she panted. "About like carrying a couple of milk jugs."

Reaching the middle of the pasture, I dropped the bucket with a thud, then flexed my hand and arm a few times. I tried not to look at the low mound at the far end, nor the flat memorial stone resting on its top. I looked anyway. I always did.

Perry leaned the shield against her leg. "Thinking about El Cid?"

"Yeah." I managed a grin and rapped the shield with my knuckles. It clanged softly. "This kind of stuff was his jam. He would've already gone into a lecture about metallurgy or one of our ancestors or other facts that nobody cares about, being all Professor Trivia."

"Right there with you. My mom's a scientist, remember?" She scratched under her cap, then tugged it back into place and glanced around. "Can I ask you something?"

"Sure."

"Your family's been here for hundreds of years, right? So why doesn't anyone in town know what you guys *really* do out here?"

"Because," Turk curled his lip, "they're clueless idiots."

Izzie sniffed. "Takes one to know one."

Rigo chuffed.

"Oh, a few of them know." Dad rolled back his sleeves, then picked up the shield and examined the grips, giving each of them a tug. "The older ones. The ones who knew my parents or have heard the same rumors too many times to discount them. Our mayor, Inez Ortega, most likely knows as well, but she pretends otherwise. We do not have a place in her worldview. However." He slid an arm through the first grip, grasped the second one in his left hand, then raised the shield. "We have found over the centuries that it is better to keep a low profile. Safer for others. Safer for us."

Talking horses and magical weapons and creatures that go bump in the night are all just too much for the average person to believe in, El Cid had explained to me once. *And what people don't understand, they fear. And what they fear, they often grow to hate.*

Perry leaned against Izzie's chest and looped an arm around the mare's neck. "Well, *I'm* glad Mom and I know." She patted Izzie, who lipped her ball cap, knocking it askew. "Talk about living the dream."

"Let us begin." Swinging his right arm, Dad walked about twenty yards away, then turned and raised both mace and shield. "Perry. When you are ready."

I backed away, then joined Rigo, taking advantage of his shadow.

The bay eyed her. "Is she good at pitching?"

"Probably. She's good at everything."

Perry plucked the softball out of the bucket. Holding the ball level with her chin in both hands, she stared at my father, eyes narrowed. With a grunt, she whipped her arm around and took a step forward, all in one motion. The ball screamed toward Dad.

"Whoa," I breathed.

Dad swung and missed, staggering a little to one side. I could tell the weight of the shield was throwing off his balance. Apprehension crept up on me. Maybe our strategy was just too far out there, even for us. He hoisted the shield again and nodded.

Perry threw a baseball this time. Dad swung again. And again, he missed. *Bong*. The ball struck the shield's edge, twisting it and his arm to one side. Saying something under his breath, he lowered the weapons for a moment, shook out his arm, then took a fresh grip and raised them back up.

"Again, Perry. As quickly as you can."

One by one, she went through the balls. And each one was a swing and a miss on Dad's scorecard. My heart dropped to my boot heels as I jogged around, shagging the balls.

An hour and five rounds with the balls later, Perry threw the last one. Dad managed to hit it. *Pure luck*, I thought, keeping that opinion to myself.

"Um, Mr. Del Toro?" Perry pointed at the bucket. "All we got left are rocks and I really don't want to throw *those* at you." She snagged a water bottle from the nearby pile, took a swig, then passed it to me.

"This isn't working, Javier," Turk called. "Let's take a break and re-think this whole strategy. C'mon, I'll give you a lift back to the house."

Dad blew out a long breath, chest heaving. Sweat darkened his shirt. Joining us, he dropped the shield to the ground. *Clang*. The mace followed. Tugging his shirttail free, he blotted his face. "I simply need more practice." He took the bottle from me, drained it, then wiped his beard. "A short rest, yes, then we will try again. I still have time to hone my technique—"

"Less than a full day," Turk interrupted. "Less than a full day to master a skill you've never done before and against an enemy that'll do her level best to kill you."

Dad stiffened. A mix of anger and betrayal flitted across his face. He raised his chin. "I am sad to know, my friend, that you have so little faith in my abilities."

Turk flipped his tail in an equine shrug. "Not to disrespect you, but going *mano a mano* with a sorceress waving a ray gun isn't part of your skill set."

Talk about harsh. I winced at Turk's bluntness.

"I'll… um… I'll collect the balls." Perry darted away, Izzie on her heels.

"I still think *I* should practice, too." I nudged the shield with my toe. "What would it hurt?"

"Matt's got a point, Javier," the black said. "You need backup and he's better than nothing."

I blinked. Had Turk the Jerk just agreed with me? "See, Dad? Even Turk thinks—"

"I said no already," Dad snapped. "Matt, we promised Liz that her daughter would be safe. You will be of more help to me by keeping Perry and the horses behind those wards." He stepped to the stallion's side. "I will accept that offer of a lift, Turk. That is, if you think I am capable of mounting without a saddle."

Turk snorted, both at the words and the tone.

"But Dad—"

Ignoring me, my father swung onto the stallion's back and settled into place. "My weapon, *por favor.*" He held out a hand. I passed him the mace. "And the shield."

I squinted at him. "I thought you were going to practice some more."

"I am, but I will not leave Santiago's shield lying in the dirt."

Jaw clenched, I picked it up. *This isn't going to work,* I wanted to yell at him. *Maybe Ben was right, and we should just give her the coffer. After all, it's sealed tight...* Frowning, I paused. A plan—a straight up *loco* one—slipped inside my skull and took a seat.

Oh.

Oh!

"Matt? The shield?"

"Uh, yeah. Here you go." I hoisted it up to him. "You know, you're right—Perry comes first."

"Yes, she does."

I kicked at the ground, digging up an innocent clump of grass as the plan unfolded inside my head. "Say, Dad? I'm, um, I'm going to hang out here awhile longer." I looked around, trying to think of a reason. My gaze landed on Perry and Izzie. *Close enough.* "Perry wants to try riding bareback and asked me to give her some pointers. Well, me and Izzie."

"Remind Isabel to go slowly at first. Turk? When you are ready." The black broke into a slow jog and started across the field.

Joining me, Rigo rested his chin on my shoulder. "You're up to something."

One eye on my father, I nodded. "I've got an idea."

16

"W ait." Perry wrinkled her face. "Say that part of your plan again?"

"Which part?" I asked.

"The stupid part where you get killed."

"Look." I crossed my arms across my chest. "If I open the Red Casket *inside the Maze* and release that thing, it'll be stuck *inside the Maze*. Get it? It won't be a threat to anyone. Then, I'll re-seal the coffer and call Hester Lemprey. I still got her card." I slapped my back pocket. "She gives us the money, then leaves with an empty coffer. No harm, no foul."

"Finally." Rigo flipped his forelock out of his eyes. "Someone sees it my way."

"Why'd you change your mind, Matt?" Izzie asked.

"C'mon. You saw how crappy Dad did today." I waved a hand toward the house. "He's going to get hurt trying to destroy her wand. Or worse." I wouldn't let myself think about that "worse" part. "You guys know Dad'll never go along with this plan, so I gotta try *something*." Why did making the hard choice feel so wrong?

"Back to the stupid part." Perry jabbed a finger into my chest. "What if that thing in the chest tries to kill you the moment you open it?"

"I don't think it will." *I hope.* "Once free, it'll just take off. And anyway, I'll be mounted. Rigo'll take care of me." I bumped his shoulder with mine. "Right?"

"As rain." He clopped his lips. "Or is it *rein*?"

"Let's say that all works out and you hand over the coffer," Perry said. "What happens if Hester Lemprey manages to open it and finds out you tricked her?"

"She can't open it—that's the beauty of this plan. I don't know why I didn't think of it before. See, Dad mentioned a few days ago that the only thing that can open a coffer is one of our maces. Not a rock or a hammer or pry bar or anything. I bet not even her fireballs could do the trick. Basically, she's buying a door stop." I glanced across the field. "But I've got to hurry before Dad notices me and Rigo are gone."

Perry and Izzie exchanged looks. Then, Perry nodded. "Right. We're in."

"Actually, I need you two to stay here and ride around and pretend to be practicing—"

"Why does Matt always do that?" Izzie asked Perry. "Try to dump us just when things get interesting?"

"I don't know, but it's getting old." Perry stepped back from Izzie's left side, took two running steps, then threw herself on the mare, landing on her stomach. With a grunt, she wiggled higher, than flung a leg over. "Yeah, yeah, I know. Awkward. But, hey, it got the job done." She pulled her cap lower and gathered two fistfuls of mane.

"You can't come with us," I groaned. "You've got to stay here and play decoy. Plus, Rigo and I might need to hightail it out of there. And you're not exactly a strong bareback rider."

"She's better than you think," Izzie said. "And anyway, I'm not about to let anything happen to her."

"Matt." Rigo nosed me. "We're losing our window. Ride now and argue later. Let's roll."

"If this is what being in charge is like, I resign." I flung myself up on Rigo, managing to knee him in the flank this time. "Sorry. Again." I scooted into place and wrapped a hank of mane around my left hand; my mace balanced across his withers. "Okay, head toward the far end of the field. Act natural."

Rigo flicked an ear. "How?"

"I don't know… trot casual."

Perry laughed.

As the horses walked toward the far end of the field, making sure to angle toward the road at the same time, I pretended to talk to Perry, who nodded and acted like she was listening. At the field's edge, I peeked over a shoulder. "Okay, the barn's blocking us. Go!"

The horses broke into a lope. Leaning forward, Perry clung to Izzie's mane, knuckles white and mouth set as she bounced with every stride.

"Relax," I hollered. "And sit up straighter. Yeah, there you go."

I glanced back as the horses galloped along the road. *Hope Dad doesn't spot our dust.* Luckily, the breeze was blowing the cloud eastward.

After a while, I tugged on Rigo's mane. "I think we're clear."

The horses eased to a trot, then jog, ribs rising and falling. Reaching the museum's sign, we checked behind as we turned onto the overgrown road. No sign of pursuit.

With the lonely mesa growing larger and larger as we jogged toward it, I argued with myself about putting Perry in possible danger. Again. But the boot leather truth was that I was glad she was with me. Why? Because I was a big ol' chicken. I'd never been inside the Maze by myself, and yeah, I needed her—and Rigo and Izzie—beside me.

A good friend rides with you. A *really* good friend rides into the Maze with you.

The horses halted outside the Gate, the cool breeze wafting over us. Circling the air with their noses, they sniffed deeply, ears flicking back and forth.

Rigo stomped once. "Skinner free as far as I can tell."

"Here we go." I squeezed my legs.

Entering the corridor, I blinked, my eyes complaining about going from bright sun to dim shadow. The horses trotted side by side; the only sound was the echoing clink of steel horseshoe on stone and the sigh of wind through the passage.

It seemed to take forever to travel the forty yards into the Maze. Not that I minded because it dawned on me that I might be freeing something that maybe, just maybe, we couldn't outrun. I shoved that thought away.

Slowing to a walk, the horses emerged into the light and stop. The sun felt comforting after the coolness of the corridor.

Perry craned her neck and scanned the area. "Not much different, even after two months. Still just as clown creepy."

I nodded. Even creepier since I didn't have Dad or Ben or El Cid to tell me what to do. I looked around, wishing I was anywhere else. I heard Mongolia was pretty cool.

Below the horses' hooves, the ground sloped down a short incline before hitting the valley's floor. Boulders and rocks, along with scrubby bushes and clumps of prairie grass, littered the three-square-mile area surrounded by towering sandstone and granite walls. The cliff faces were slashed here and there by narrow slot canyons, most of them unexplored.

An abandoned dirt road led to remnants of a camp tucked in the southwest corner of the valley: the paleontologists' former work site. Even though the trailers and most of the tents had been removed last month, there were still bits of leftover junk.

Perry shifted on Izzie's back. "Mom would go berserk if she knew what we were doing right now." She fiddled with the reins. "Now that I'm here, I'm feeling a little freaked myself."

Not as much as I am. "Let's get this over with. The cave's that way." I pointed my chin toward the northeast corner of the valley. "We'll grab the Red Casket and bring it closer to the Gate. Then, it's open, release, re-seal, and ride like heck out of here."

Perry grinned weakly. "I like that last part the best."

"Hey, Per?" Izzie stepped to the edge of the slope. "Lean back a little until I reach the bottom. Legs tight, okay?"

"Got it." She hunkered back, feet slightly forward, and both hands braced on the mare's withers.

Izzie eased down the slope. Rigo followed. Reaching the valley floor, they broke into a steady lope. Even though I knew the skinners were locked away in the larger coffer, I kept my mace ready and my head on a pivot the whole way. Sure, there was only a whistle-thin chance that a few of those hamburger horrors hadn't been rounded up, but still.

By the time we reached the cave, both horses were blowing hard; Rigo's sweat soaked the bottom of my jeans. We sighed in relief as we rode into the cliff's shadow.

Perry removed her cap and fanned her face. Her short hair stuck out in all directions. "Where's the cave?"

Swinging my right leg over Rigo's neck, I grimaced at the sticky feel of wet denim and slid to the ground. "Behind that."

That being an enormous slab of sandstone. Resting on one edge, it tilted against the cliff, forming an opening one-person wide at the bottom before tapering sharply to the top. "The cave's back in there."

My pulse kicked into high gear. Squeezing behind that slab was bad enough. But then I'd have to crawl through a tight tunnel to even reach the cave. On my belly. With no light. I swallowed, mouth suddenly Death Valley–dry. Oh boy.

Perry dismounted, landing with an *oof.* "You know." She walked over and peered behind the block. "I've always wondered what that cave looked like. Let me go back there, Matt, and get the coffer. You told me Roman stored the thing just inside the opening. How hard can it be?"

"Nah, I'll do it." *Just as soon as I work up the nerve.*

"Why? It's not that big. If I can't carry it, I'll drag it out."

I swallowed again, bile burning my throat. "My job, not yours." I let out a shaky breath, and took an even shaki- er step forward

"Oops, too late." She darted behind the slab and disap- peared. "If you follow me, Matt Del Toro," she called, her voice echoing, "I'll sic Izzie on you."

Centuries passed. Then, she re-appeared, dusty and car- rying the Red Casket clutched to her chest with both arms. "It's heavier than it looks," she gasped.

I helped her lower the coffer to the ground. About the size and shape of an extra-large shoebox—the kind boots came in—the iron surface was scratched and dulled from centuries of hard living. The metal had a reddish-brown tint like the color of a dried scab.

Slapping sand off her clothes, Perry nudged the chest with the toe of her boot. "So that's *El Cofre Rojo.* Did I pronounce it right? And, please, don't tell me that's dried blood on it. Because ewww."

Izzie nosed it. "Smells like skinner leftover."

"You're probably smelling the other coffer." I unbuck- led my belt and slid it free from my jeans. "Did you see it, by the way?"

"The other chest? Yeah." Perry nodded. "Still in there. Doesn't look like anything got out, if that's what you're asking. I mean, I didn't see any tracks or anything. And it had a layer of dust on the lid."

"Good. One less thing to worry about." I squatted down. Wrapping my belt around the chest, I just managed to fasten the buckle on the last hole. "Give me a hand." With Perry's help, I placed the coffer on Rigo's broad haunch. Using a nearby rock, I mounted carefully, then reached back with one hand and slid my fingers under the leather strap. I sure could've used a saddle.

"You okay, Rigo? It's not digging into you or anything?"

He shifted from hoof to hoof. "I'll live."

"Okay, then." I nodded at Perry already astride Izzie. "Let's go free a monster."

17

At the bottom of the incline below the Gate, we stood in a circle and peered down at the Red Casket. The sun blazed down and turned the valley into a kiln; the towering walls blocked any chance of a breeze. I blamed the weather, not my nerves, on the sweat beading on my forehead.

Lowering his head until his nose almost touched the thing, Rigo cocked his head. "Hmm."

"Do you hear something?" I edged closer.

"Sort of." He tilted his head the other way. "Sounds like that mice colony. The one that's taken over the barn? Only this sounds… *bigger*."

"There are *mice*?" Perry's eyes widened. "In the *barn*?"

Izzie listened, too. "Yeah, like a rat. Hey, maybe that's what you saw earlier, Matt. Instead of a hand, it was a giant rat's paw."

"Um, guys." Perry inched backwards, an odd expression on her face. "Not a fan of rodents, especially ones with naked tails, so, if you don't mind, I'll just be over here."

"No, wait." I said. "Mount up instead. Izzie, you and Perry get behind those rocks." I pointed my mace at a nearby jumble of boulders, each one the size of a bus. "I'm not sure how bad the blast will be when I open it. And, Izzie, if things go south…"

"I know, I know. Flee. Run away. Get Perry to safety. Yadda, yadda, yadda." Still complaining, she and Perry disappeared behind the boulders.

Removing my belt, I tossed it to one side and hoisted the coffer onto a nearby boulder the height of Rigo's chest. I pushed it into place, making sure it was secure, then scrambled back up on Rigo.

My war-brother took a position sideways to the coffer. Good thinking. I wrapped a fistful of mane around my left hand and tightened my legs. His whole body tensed, ready to bolt.

"Hey, Rigo. Don't run out from under me, okay? I'd hate to be left behind with that thing."

"When have I ever dumped you?" One ear pointed back at me like an accusing finger.

"Like a bazillion times. You're like riding a jackrabbit without a saddle and—"

"Matt, quit stalling already," Izzie called, "and get on with it. We've got to get back before Javier gets suspicious."

"Close your eyes, Rigo." Raising my mace over my head, I took a deep breath, my fingers digging into the leather-wrapped haft.

"SANTIAGO!" The war cry burst from my chest. I slammed my mace down on the edge of the lid as hard I could. The booming clang rattled my teeth. Face scrunched, I waited for a blast of light.

Nothing. Just a faint blue-white gleam along the lid's seam. It flared briefly, then faded. *Snick.* The lid popped free, opening a crack.

My breath caught somewhere between lungs and mouth, I leaned closer.

The coffer leaped off the boulder, lid flapping like a bird's wing. For a nano-second, I caught a glimpse of a human-like creature with a mane of scraggly white hair and skeleton-skinny arms and legs covered with leathery skin. One arm looked like it had been gnawed on; the white bone gleamed through the ragged flesh. The creature's mouth was stretched wide and yellow teeth filled its maw as it shrieked in a rising screech that never stopped. I felt like my ears were going to burst.

The creature barreled into me. My head snapped back. Stunned by the impact, I slid sideways, clutching the stallion's mane with one hand and a leg hooked over his back. Rigo twisted as he fought to stay between me and the ground. Gasping in terror, I clawed my way back up.

Chest heaving and mace at the ready, I tried to look in all four directions at once. Nothing, but rocks and bushes and the coffer upside down on the ground. I sucked in a breath, then another, ordering my heart to rein it in.

With Perry crouched over her neck, Izzie trotted up. "Holy molasses, that scream almost split my skull. What was that thing?" She shook her head, mane flying, then peered around. "And where'd it go?"

"Don't know and don't know." Rigo said, tail lashing his hindquarters. "I was busy keeping Matt from kissing the dirt."

"I'm guessing," Perry eyed the coffer, "that wasn't a rat."

"No, it was kind of…" I thought for a moment, "Gollum-like. But with all this crazy white hair and with dried up, leathery skin. Bad teeth."

"So, like an Orc?" Perry guessed.

"Close, but more skeleton-y. Ent-ish."

"Do *you* know what they're talking about?" Izzie asked Rigo.

He shook his head. "Not a clue."

I swung a leg over and slid to the ground. "Now for the hard part."

Perry grimaced. "That wasn't the hard part?"

"Not even close."

I wish I had some aspirin. Because sealing the casket back up was going to hurt. A lot. I walked over to the chest, wedged my mace under one edge, and flipped it upright. The lid flopped open; the creak of the hinges sounded a lot like the creature's shriek.

"What are *those*?" Perry pointed at the coffer. "On the inside of the lid. Those scratch marks."

"Guess whatever was inside didn't like tight places any more than I do." A few of the gouges looked fresh. For a moment, pity filled me. *Except it wouldn't have been locked up in the first place if it didn't deserve it.* I started to close the lid, then paused and leaned closer.

In the center of the inside of the lid, the scratches looked deeper, as if they had been etched over and over. I squinted at them. For a moment, I thought the marks formed a pattern: a diamond bisected with a vertical line. I stared harder. Nah, maybe not. The scratches were just from the creature trying to claw its way out.

I shuddered, then kicked the lid shut. *Thunk.*

"Okay, I want everyone back behind the rocks again," I ordered. "Yeah, even you, Rigo. You three make sure that creature doesn't sneak back, okay? Last thing we need is a surprise attack. Although, the way it skedaddled, I think it just wanted to get as far away from us as possible." *I hope.* I waved them away.

I waited until the tip of Rigo's tail vanished, then scraped a burr-free spot in the dirt. My new strategy: drop and duck. Knees bent and shoulders hunched in anticipation, I grasped the mace in both hands and pointed it at the empty casket.

"*Stamus contra malum.*" I whispered the phrase Dad had taught us earlier in the summer when he showed Ben and me how to seal a coffer. Nothing happened. I cleared my throat and tried again. "*Stamus contra malum.*"

A low hum began. It vibrated from the mace and up my arms. It grew strong, as if the weapon was trying to shake free. Gritting my teeth, I tightened my grip and stretched my arms out. *Please let this work.*

"*Stamus contra malum!*" I shouted and rapped the coffer with my mace.

The same flash of blue-white light. Squeezing my eyes, I hit the dirt and curled over my knees into a ball. Even so, the blast bowled me over. Breathless, I sprawled on the ground, still clinging to my mace. Grit and pebbles stung my face and arms. Then, an odd quiet. I waited a few heartbeats, then cracked an eye.

The casket was bathed in a neon glow. As I watched, the light faded, returning the iron to its reddish hue. I opened my other eye. Good. The lid was sealed tight as a cinch on a bronco.

"Matt!" Perry sprinted over and skidded to a stop beside me. The warhorses crowded behind her. "You okay?" She grabbed my arm. With a grunt, she hauled me to my feet. "Wow. I felt it right through my legs and everything."

"Should've been at ground zero." I grimaced and rubbed my temple.

Snuffling, Rigo stuck his nose in my face. "How bad?"

"About what I expected. And stop slobbering on me, dude." I pushed him away with a pat. "Perry? Find my belt and—"

"Got it." She darted off.

With Perry's help, I got the casket—and myself—back on Rigo. My temples throbbed with each move. Reaching back, I grasped the strap, then pressed a heel against the warhorse's side.

Head low, Rigo plodded up the incline. Inside the corridor, he broke into a gentle jog, shuffling along like he was carrying an egg on his back.

He's worse than El Cid, I thought. "Sheesh, Rigo, my head doesn't hurt *that* much. You don't have to be so careful."

"Just doing my job."

I grinned and laid my hand on his shoulder. Beneath my palm, his muscles bunched and flowed under the glossy coat. Next to us, Perry rode lightly, moving in rhythm with

Izzie's stride, head up, heels down, and fingers twined in the sorrel's mane.

Realization, as warm and bright and promise filled as the morning sun, welled up inside of me. I may have lost El Cid, but I gained three good friends. Three *best* friends. Guess the universe considered it a fair trade.

Yeah, I could live with that.

We rode for the exit in silence. Once outside the Maze, Izzie and Rigo halted, blowing and shaking their heads. Equine tension relief.

"So." Perry pushed her cap higher. "We just *phone* her? Hey, Hester? We're calling to let you know your order's ready for pick up."

I shrugged. "It's not like I've done this kind of thing before." With my free hand, I fished out the sorceress's business card and my cell phone. I entered the number, then put the call on speaker. It rang twice.

"Who is this?" Hester Lemprey sounded annoyed. "How did you get this number?"

"This is Matt Del Toro. And you gave it to me yesterday." I took a deep breath. "I've got the Red Casket."

A long pause. "Wait. *You've* got it. Not your daddy?"

"What does it matter? You want it or not?"

A longer pause. "When and where."

"Right now. At the Maze. Where we met yesterday." In the background, I caught the thump of boots, then a door opening and closing.

"Be there in ten. Oh, and kid? If you do an end run around me, what happens afterwards will be *your* fault. Payback is something I'm really, *really* good at." *Beep.* The call ended.

Legs trembling, I stood over the casket, mace in hand and eyes on the sorceress. Both warhorses flanked me, their necks arched and nostrils flared. Equine bodyguards. And, to my utter and jaw-dropping astonishment, Perry had agreed to stay near the Gate, just a step away from the protection of the wards.

"I want Izzie and Rigo concentrating on keep you safe, Matt," Perry had said, "not worrying about me. Although I don't know what's worse," she had added as she took up her position, "facing that screecher creature *inside* the Maze, or a wacko witch *outside* the Maze."

A few yards away, Hester Lemprey waited beside her bike, crystal leveled at me. The only sound was the growl of the idling motor. Her eyes gleamed as she stared at the coffer. "If that's not the *real* Red Casket, then you're dead meat."

"Well, it is."

"Bring it closer." She beckoned me with her free hand.

I took a step forward, then paused. "Show me the money first."

She reached inside her jacket and pulled out a thick manila envelope. A heavy rubber band was wrapped around it. "Thirty thousand. Cash." She tossed it halfway between us.

I picked up the chest and carried it over. *Did it feel lighter? Would she be able to tell it was empty?* Keeping one eye on her, I set it on the ground next to the envelope, then scooped up the package and backed away until I bumped into Rigo.

Her crystal still aimed at me, Hester Lemprey did the same. Except she was able to hoist the coffer up with one arm. The big show-off. She stored it inside one of the saddle bags. "Feel free to count the money." Her lip curled. "Never trust a witch, right?"

I pulled off the rubber band and opened the envelope. Stacks of one hundred dollar bills were bundled together with paper strips. My heart leaped. I imagined all the things I could buy. A new cell phone. A car for Ben. Get Dad's truck fixed up. *Dude*, I reminded myself. *Stay focused.* I pretended to count them, hoping I looked like I knew what I was doing. Not like I had ever seen thirty thousand dollars in one place before. I looked up and nodded once.

"I'm outta here." Hester Lemprey swung a leg over the bike. "Tell Javier that I kept my word." She revved the engine, then roared away. Dust hung in the air before slinking off.

Perry hurried over. "'Ding, dong, the witch is gone.' Too bad it isn't permanently."

I blew out a long breath, then slumped against my war-brother. "And *we're* still alive."

"We better get back." Rigo nudged me. "Mount up."

Approaching the ranch at a steady lope, I kept my gaze locked on the field and the house beyond. The horses, too, their ears pinned forward. Reaching the edge of the field, they slowed to a walk.

"So far, so good," Izzie muttered.

"Matt." Perry held out her hand. "Give me the money." She pulled off her hat, packed the envelope inside of it, then tucked the cap under one arm.

I blinked. "Smart."

She nodded. "Parental subterfuge—another one of my superpowers."

As we neared the barn, I caught the *ping, ping, ping* of Dad's shoeing hammer. We rounded the corner of the building. In the yard, Turk stood on three legs. Bent over, my father clasped the black's right hind fetlock between his knees as he drove a nail into Turk's hoof. Perry winced.

Letting go of the stallion's leg, Dad rose with a groan, arching his back. "Better?"

Turk stomped his hoof a few times. "Yeah. Thanks."

"And how was your ride, *mija*? More of a challenge?" My father smiled up at Perry. Collecting his tools, he tossed them inside a bucket with a ringing clang and picked it up.

"In so many ways. But I'm getting the hang of it." She swung her right leg over Izzie's neck, and slid off. "Whew, it's hot. Think I'll get some water. Be right back." Hat clamped tightly under her arm, she scooted into the house.

Wow. She's good. "You guys need anything?" I asked Rigo as I dismounted. Izzie was already nostril-deep in the water barrel.

"Not a thing." Rigo gave me a meaningful shove toward the house with his nose.

As soon as Dad disappeared inside the barn with his tools, I sprinted for the house and hurried down the hall to Ben's room. The door was closed.

"Hey." I knocked once. "It's me."

"Come in."

Perry knelt by her large duffle, shoving clothes and her tablet to one side. As I watched, she stuffed the envelope under a pile of socks and underwear. "Less chance of your dad coming across it here with my stuff."

"Make that *no* chance."

"Now what do we do?" She sat back on her heels.

My stomach grumbled. "Um… lunch?"

᠙᠊᠙

"I still can't believe I pulled it off," I said. "I mean, *we* pulled it off."

After lunch, Perry and I retreated to Ben's room, pretending to watch my well-used copy of *The Fellowship of the Rings* on my brother's ancient TV attached to a slightly less ancient DVD player. All my *The Lord of the Rings* stuff—from the old DVDs to the action figures—were originally my mom's. I always wondered if I was such a fan because I knew *she* had been.

Stretched out on the floor, I clasped my hands behind my head and sighed. "Got rid of Hester Lemprey *and* scored a big-time bonus." I grinned at the ceiling. "What should I get? New cell, for sure. Oh, and Per? Half the money is yours, you know."

"Are you kidding?" Sitting cross-legged on the bed, Perry snorted. "I was just along for the ride. Plus, I'd have to confess to Mom where it came from if I ever wanted to spend any of it. Thanks, but hard pass." With the door ajar, she kept her voice low. We had closed it earlier, but Dad made us open it. Still, she lowered it even more. "Um, Matt? How are you going to tell your father what we did?"

"I don't know." My good mood dried up. "I think I'll wait until—"

A distant chime. My father's cell phone. His voice drifted from the living room as he spoke to someone. Yeah, we both totally listened. I heard him say "Victoria."

"C'mon." I scrambled to my feet and hurried along the hall, Perry right behind me.

Leaning back in his chair, Dad sat with boots propped on the desk; rank really did have its privileges. A woman's voice spoke from the cell phone in front of him. Spotting us, he waved us closer. Perry sat in the other chair while I perched on a corner of the desk, swinging a leg.

"Victoria? Say again, *por favor*?"

"I have more information about Hester Lemprey," the hunter said over the rustle of paper. I imagined her long, narrow face framed with shoulder-length hair, dark brown strands streaked with gray, pulled back at the nape of her neck. "There is a strong possibility she can open our coffers given enough time and access to certain dark resources."

My lungs stopped. A cold chill danced up and down my spine. I leaned closer to the phone, mouth dry. "L-like *how* strong a possibility, Victoria?"

A pause. "Matt? Is that *you*?" The hunter laughed. "Why, you sound like your brother. How long has it been? Two years? Almost three? Is Ben there, too?"

"No, he is at the Navarre ranch right now," my father said, "helping Josefina."

"Oh, *sí*. Helping." Victoria chuckled. "Javier, you need to load up your boys and come down to Arizona for a long visit. Take a break from those Colorado winters."

"*Gracias*, we will try," Dad said. "Especially if we live through the rest of this summer, no?" He winked at Perry, who managed a weak smile.

"Speaking of not dying, there is something else you should know," Victoria continued. Another crinkle of paper. "This is not the first time those wand-wielders have wanted our coffers. Years ago, a coven of sorceresses—"

"No, coven is just for witches," Perry blurted out. "A group of sorcerers or sorceresses is called a secret." Her cheeks flushed when we stared at her. "What? Collective nouns are cool."

"So this secret of sorceresses," Victoria continued, a hint of amusement in her voice, "tried unsuccessfully to steal as many coffers as they could. They fled after they re-learned the old lesson that they were no match for us Knights."

"Why did they want our coffers?" Dad asked the question before I could. "They could not open them. And even if they had found a way, what about the creatures inside? Would they not attack the sorceresses?"

If only, I thought to myself.

"Apparently, they had crafted a weapon or tool of some sort that enabled them to control those *monstruos*. And we both know, Javier, the first thing our enemy would have done was set loose every skinner, fire drake, sand demon, *duende*—and whatever other horrors were imprisoned inside—upon the nearest Knights and their families. The sorceresses' desire for revenge has not diminished over time. No, it has traveled down the centuries, passing from one generation to the next."

Revenge? Perry asked me silently.

I'll explain later, I mouthed back.

"What became of this weapon?" Dad asked.

"The Knights were able to seize it. They could not destroy it, so they hid it away for safekeeping. From what I have read, and after conversations with several older hunters, I am fairly certain the weapon was sealed in one of our coffers." She barked a laugh. "I will give you three guesses as to which one."

Swinging his boots down with a thud, Dad lurched upright in his chair. "*El Cofre Rojo*. So, *that* is why Hester Lemprey wants it so badly." He shook his head. "And after declaring there is nothing dangerous inside. See, my son? This is why you can never trust a witch."

I barely heard him over the thud of my heart. *What did I do? What was I thinking, handing over the Red Casket to her?* Then, relief flooded me, leaving me so weak I almost melted off the desk and onto the floor.

There wasn't anything inside, I reminded myself. *Just that whatever-it-is. And it's probably cowering in the back of a slot canyon.* I shot a peek at Perry. Her expression was a hard-fought neutral, but her eyes were wide. I tried to recall if I had seen anything else inside the casket beside that creature. *I don't think there was. And Rigo would've mentioned it if he had seen something.* I shook myself and refocused on the conversation.

"I know you re-sealed that coffer earlier this summer," Victoria was saying, "and I do not mean to tell you how to run things, but it might be a good idea to double-check it. Just to make sure. Of course, as long as *El Cofre Rojo* is locked up and hidden in the Maze and behind the wards, all will be fine."

"A failed seal. That is all we need right now." Dad rubbed the back of his neck. "I will ride out this afternoon. I am also thinking of moving the coffer to a different hiding place inside the Maze until I have dealt with Hester Lemprey."

"Listen, I know you are stretched thin with Ben being away," Victoria said. "If you need us, my sisters and I can make your ranch in a day. We will even bring a cousin or two to help."

"I will not hesitate to call, Victoria."

"Ah, Javier, you are such a liar. And do not forget—I want to see you down south sooner than later, okay? *Buena suerte, mi amigo.*"

Face thoughtful as the call ended, Dad leaned back, his chair creaking. "I will follow her advice and make a quick visit to the Maze this afternoon. Since Turk will be with me, there is no need for Isabel and Rigo... *Matt?* What is wrong, my son? Are you ill?"

I opened my mouth, but the only thing that came out was a garbled noise. I felt lightheaded as the blood in my face drained away. Out of the corner of my eye I noticed Perry clutching the chair's wooden arms, her knuckles white.

"You can't go to the Maze." Real words finally showed up. "You need to… I mean… you should stay here and… and…" Pulse roaring in my ears, I looked at Perry. *Help me!*

"And practice with the shield," she blurted. "Yeah. That's it. More practice. Like for *hours.*"

"I do not believe that strategy is going to work after all." Dad sighed. "As Turk pointed out, it is not in my skill set."

Perry and I stared at each other. I swallowed, then stood up, hands braced on the desk. Just in case my knees failed me.

Frowning, Dad straightened. His eyes narrowed. "All right, you two. What is going on? And, please, skip the creative obfuscating and tell me."

"You can't go check on the Red Casket, Dad." My lips were so stiff I could barely form the words.

"And why is that?"

"Because it's gone. I sold it to Hester Lemprey."

"Y OU WHAT?" Dad leaped to his feet. His chair rolled back and crashed into the bookshelf. His mouth opened and closed a few times. "When? How?"

"Earlier today. I-I rode out there and—"

"*We* rode there," Perry said.

"—and grabbed the coffer and carried it out of the Maze, then I called her." I decided mentioning the part where I opened the chest could wait. Like until I was in my late twenties, early thirties. "She gave me her number yesterday." Pulling the business card from my pocket, I placed it on the desk. "We got the money, by the way."

The muscles in his jaws twitched. He started to say something, then gave up—probably because Perry was present. Stepping around the desk, he crossed the living room in three strides, and slapped the screen door open. It cracked against the side of the house, then whapped shut. His boots pounded the wooden treads as he stormed away.

I let out a shaky breath. So did Perry.

Eying the door, I said, "Stay here, okay?"

"I'll go with you," Perry offered.

"Thanks, but I got this." Forcing my legs to move, I slipped outside and glanced around. No sign of anyone. A hollow *thud* from the barn. Then another. Like Turk was trying to kick his way through the back door. I followed the sound.

Beams of light slanted from the tiny windows over the barn's loft. One beam was a spotlight, illuminating the shield propped against a straw bale. My father stood in the middle of the barn, his back to me. The bucket of balls from earlier sat by his boots. As I watched, he reached down and grabbed a rock, then hurled it as hard as he could at the back wall. *Thunk*. It bounced off the wall and spun away into the shadows.

"Dad."

"I am busy." He picked up another rock and let it fly. *Thunk*. Splinters of wood flew into the air, leaving white gouges in the aged boards.

"I know you're mad at me, Dad, but I thought—"

"No." He whirled around, eyes blazing. "No, you did *not* think. What you did was make the situation worse than before. You heard what Victoria said about the sorceresses' weapon."

Oh, right. My strategy blew apart like a house of cards in a high wind. I did have one ace to play, so I laid it on the table. "Actually, the situation is *better* than before." I shifted from foot to foot. "I, uh, I opened the casket before I handed it over."

Dad's jaw sagged. "You opened the casket?"

"Yeah. But there wasn't any tool or weapon inside. Just some creature. Like a hag or something. It—or she, I'm not sure which—took off as soon as it was free. And there wasn't anything else in the casket. No wand or crystal or *anything*."

"Wait." Dad frowned. "Nothing at all?"

I shook my head. "Ask Rigo. He was right there with me. Just that hag or whatever it is. And now it's trapped in the Maze, so that's a good thing, right? I re-sealed the casket like you showed us earlier this summer. So even if Hester Lemprey *does* figure out how to open it, there's nothing inside. It's empty."

"And if she does manage to open it?" Worry tightened the skin around his eyes. "What then?"

"What do you mean?"

"Do you not think she will come after us? We will always be looking over our shoulders. Never knowing when Hester Lemprey will retaliate. Tell me, my son, is that how you wish to live your life?"

"At least we'd be alive."

"Alive and living are not the same, Matt." He raised his arms in frustration. "Did you not think through the ramifications?"

"Of course I did." *Sort of.* "It's not my first rodeo, Dad. Anyway, I thought you wanted me to take over the ranch. Make decisions. Start running things." Resentment flared up, flamed by the complete and total conviction that I had royally screwed up, I had tried to do the right thing and had flubbed it. Big time. "That's what *you said*," I yelled. My pulse roared in my ears, making my voice sound far away.

"I did not mean starting *this week*," he shouted back. "And why, in the name of all that is holy, did you not consult me before doing something so stupid?"

"Because you would've said no." With all the yelling we were doing, a sliver of my mind wondered why the horses hadn't shown up. "You would've tried to fight her with the shield, and... and..." I couldn't say the rest of it.

Dad raised his chin. "Ah. I see. You think the *bruja* will defeat me. That my skill and experience are not enough. That you must result to trickery and lies to protect your old man."

I shrugged, suddenly tired of fighting. We rarely butted heads—that was my brother's specialty—but, when we did, I felt sick to my stomach. Like the world was tilting from side to side, and it was all I could do not to slide off the edge.

Slumping down on a nearby hay bale, I stared at my boots. "I just... I just don't want you to... to die too." Right then, I wanted El Cid so badly, it was like my heart was bleeding.

Guess Dad felt the same way. Or knew what I was feeling. He sighed, then scrubbed the back of his hand across his mouth.

"Locking horns with each other," he said in a calmer tone, "will not solve anything."

I nodded. The world slowly righted under my feet. "Do you have a plan?"

"The beginning of one, yes. Right now, however, we must assume she will return. We need to guard from a surprise attack. We need something to protect us. To stand between us and the sorceress's fireballs." As he spoke, he studied the shield, eyes narrowed in thought.

"Thought you said the shield won't work?" Frowning, I eyed it as well. "Even if we just used it for defense, it's too small for all of us to fit behind."

A corner of his mouth quirked. "Oh, I am thinking of something much, *much* larger to defend us."

ॐॐ

"Do you always hold your war councils out here?" Seated on the edge of the porch, Perry balanced a bowl of sliced up apples on her lap. The horses clustered around the bottom step, eyeing the treats. "Here, Izzie." She held out a slice to the sorrel.

"More comfortable out here than the barn." I leaned back on one elbow and stretched out my legs, grateful for the porch's shade.

"And it's not like we'd all fit inside on the sofa." Rigo flapped his lips at the bowl. "I wouldn't say no to a piece."

Munching, Izzie butted him away. "Get your own. Perry made these for *me*."

"Now, children. Play nice." Perry held out her hands, a slice on each one. "Hey, Turk? Want some? There's plenty."

Turk twitched an ear in surprise.

It dawned on me that neither Ben nor I had ever once offered a treat to Turk. Not like I did with El Cid. In fact, the gray stallion and I would ride into town a couple of times a week to the 7-Eleven for a soda—El Cid had a thing for Mountain Dew. And I knew Ben kept Izzie supplied with chilled pears, her favorite snack.

But besides Dad sometimes sharing a beer with the black stallion, did anyone really pamper Turk? Perry's earlier comment came back to me. About Turk always being on the outside of the family circle.

Maybe it was time to break that circle.

I plucked a piece out of the bowl and hopped off the porch. "Here." I held out my hand. "I mean, if you want one."

Turk paused, eyeing me through his heavy forelock, then lowered his head. His whiskers tickled my palm as he lipped up the treat and began grinding away in a sideways motion. "Thanks."

I nodded. Looking past his head, I noticed the wound on his shoulder. Had it only been a day or so since the fight between him and Rigo? Seemed like a million years. I stepped closer. "That bite looks a little swollen."

Turk swallowed. "I already told Javier it's no big deal."

"Let's keep that way. Hold on."

I jogged back up the steps and headed for the kitchen. Dad was rummaging in the fridge for a post-supper beer. Opening the drawer where we keep the first aid, I searched for the tube of antibiotic ointment.

"Someone is hurt?" Dad asked.

His matter-of-fact tone eased the worry I'd carried around all afternoon—that he might not be able to forgive my colossal screw-up. But I guess he had. Probably because he had a loose cannon of a witch to deal with. Even so, I always admired my father's ability to simply move on. Sure, he got mad about stuff, but it seemed like he could put anger and frustration to one side and focus on the *real* issue in front of him. Guess he had a lot of practice from dealing with Ben.

"Oh, just that bite on Turk's shoulder looks sketchy." I kept pawing. "I thought Kathleen re-stocked us last time she was here." The red-headed veterinarian kept us Del Toros well supplied with every kind of equine first aid. Human, too. "No, wait. Found it."

"Do you need my help?" He popped the cap off on the edge of the counter and took a long drink.

"I got this." I hurried back outside and joined Turk. Squirting the ointment on my finger, I smeared it gently into the wound. "Should've cleaned the cut first. Sorry."

"No worries."

I gave a nod, then walked back, scrubbing my hand on my jeans. Tossing the tube to one side, I took my seat on the porch just as Dad sauntered out, beer in hand. He took another swig, then waggled the bottle at Turk.

The stallion shook his mane. "Nah, I'm good, Javier."

Dad set the bottle by the rail, then walked down the steps and rested a boot on the bottom tread. "It is best we assume Hester Lemprey will find a way to open the casket. And when she discovers it is empty, she will return, seeking vengeance. Our ranch does not provide any protection, so we must leave it for now, and go where she cannot follow."

I was pretty sure I knew what he had in mind. "Good idea, but what about that creature? The one from the Red Casket." I waved a hand about. "The... whatever-it-is."

"I'm going with hag." Perry offered. "That's how I pictured it—*her*—from your description. Not very original, I know, but we have to call her *something*. Best I could come up with on short notice."

"A lone creature, we can handle," Dad said. "I am more concerned about the sorceress."

"Hey." Turk snorted. "Want to let the rest of us in on the conversation? Where are we going?"

Dad cocked an eyebrow at me. "Matt?"

I pointed north. "Into the Maze."

I poked my head into Perry's room. "Okay, Izzie's saddled and wants to know what's taking you so long."

"Funny. My mom always says the same thing." Kneeling on the floor strewn with clothes, Perry was stuffing her tablet into her day pack.

"You know there's no Wi-Fi in the Maze," I said. "We'll be lucky to get any bars on our phones."

Her hands stilled. "Well, then." She tossed the device on the bed, then shoved another hoodie into the already bulging pack and wrestled with the zipper. "Guess there's room for my toothbrush now." Rising, she stood and nudged a pair of jeans to one side, searching the floor. "Wherever it is."

"Perry." Dad appeared at the door, cell phone in hand. "I spoke with your mother. She wanted to fly back immediately, but I told her we must not give Hester Lemprey yet another target. For the time being, *she* is safer in Chicago, and *you* are safer with us."

"Yes!" Beaming, Perry hopped over the pile of clothing and hugged him. "I owe you one, Mr. Del Toro."

Dad patted her on the shoulder. "Then I will collect that debt *now*." A corner of his mouth curled.

"Oh." Her expression faltered. "Um, sure."

"We are friends, no? Then, please, call me Javier from now on, and not Mr. Del Toro. It sits more comfortably in my ears."

"Mom won't like it, but okay." Perry's grin blossomed. "Javier."

"*Bueno.*" He smiled. "And your mother would like you to call her before we leave for the Maze. Come, Matt." Dad motioned me out of the room, then ushered me down the hall and toward the kitchen.

"Did you talk to Ben?" I asked over my shoulder. "How's it going down there?"

"They are holding their own, but barely. He wanted to return home, but I told him to stay. Jo needs him. I promised him, however, that if the situation here worsens, I will take Victoria Montoya's offer. Now, are you packed?"

"Yup. And I loaded the camping gear on the horses. What about water?" Another worry worm tickled the back of my neck. Something about riding into the Maze to escape Hester Lemprey. I brushed it away. My father knew what he was doing.

"There is a seep—a natural spring—in one of the slot canyons. We will need to filter it, but it should provide enough drinking water for us and the horses. Here." He handed me a box filled with packets of freeze-dried meals, three refillable water bottles—already filled—a lone packet of Slim Jims, various snacks, and more toilet paper than we would ever use. "Find a place for all of this in the saddle-bags. Leave the box."

By the time I made repeated trips hauling and loading everything we'd need, the sun was closing in on the top of the Sangre de Cristos. In the yard, Izzie and Rigo took turns at the water barrel. Turk stood off to one side, flexing and shaking his right hind leg. I frowned. *What's up with him?*

I joined Perry on the porch, waiting for my father. She insisted on taking charge of the shield. It leaned against her knees.

"Because you know what carrying this makes me, right?" Perry ran a hand across the crescent moon.

I fought to not roll my eyes. "A shield maiden."

"I am so Rohan." Her grin faded. "By the way, what was Victoria Montoya talking about earlier? About the sorceresses' revenge and all that?"

"It's about them being sore losers." Rigo strolled over, muzzle dripping. He shook his head, slinging droplets of fresh water and not so fresh horse slobber on us. "You know how during the seventeenth century, all kinds of monsters and supernatural creatures—including a pack of sorceresses—

"A *secret* of sorceresses," Perry corrected.

"—were rampaging through Europe," he continued, "especially in Spain, attacking and killing its people? And how a band of knights joined forces and fought back and won?"

"Sure, I know the story." Perry nodded. "That was the beginning of the Order of the Knights of the Coffer." She rapped the shield; it rang softly.

"Well, the sorceresses—the ones who went to the dark side—got pretty much wiped out during that time. But a few didn't, and they swore to end the Knights no matter how long it took."

Izzie joined us. She butted Rigo with the side of her head. "You're such a nerd."

He flattened his ears. "Why? Because I know stuff?"

"No, because you assume others are interested in the stuff you know." She chuffed.

Rigo flattened his ears even more.

I hurriedly spoke up. "Good thing the Red Casket was empty, except for that hag. Guess the mysterious weapon is hidden in another coffer somewhere else."

"Unless…" Perry said slowly.

"Unless what?"

She scrunched one eye in thought. "This may sound out there, but could the *hag* be the weapon?"

I started to laugh, then paused. "That's a scary thought."

"No, she could not." Dad appeared in the doorway. He stepped outside. "That intensity of magical power must be contained within an object. Like a wand or crystal. Or our maces." He held up his weapon. "A human—or someone who was once human, such as a sorceress—cannot hold that much power. Their bodies would explode."

I made a face. "You mean *literally* explode? Like chunks of people parts all over the place?"

Dad shrugged. "Only truly supernatural beings can handle that much direct power."

"Like what?" Rigo asked. "Or rather who?"

"Angels, of course." Dad touched his chest. I knew he wore a small Saint Michael the Archangel charm on a gold chain under his shirt. "And certain demons." He studied me with a slight frown. "I have been remiss in educating you about some of the lesser-known aspects of our people. I will have to fix that. But now is not the time."

Closing the door behind him, he followed us to the horses. He waited while Perry clambered up on Izzie and settled in the saddle, then handed her the shield.

Perry slipped her right arm through the grips and rested the shield on her thigh, then gathered the reins in her left hand. "How long will we be in there?"

Dad pushed his hat back and looked up at her. "I do not know, *mija*. We have enough supplies for several days. It will depend on Hester Lemprey. Hopefully, this will be nothing more than a camping trip." He patted her knee, then laid a hand on the mare's shoulder. "Isabel?"

The sorrel tossed her head. "Don't worry. I got this."

I swung up on Rigo, maneuvering my leg around the saddle bags and over the pack tied behind the cantle. Finding my seat, I pulled my mace from the horn and looped the leather thong around my wrist, thumped my war-brother's shoulder. "Doing okay?"

"Outside of feeling like a pack burro, I'm solid."

"Javier." Turk limped over. "Hate to tell you, but that shoe is loose again. I think I picked up a stone, too."

Dad sighed. "Well, better now than on the road." He waved the black over to the barn. "Matt? You and Perry go ahead. I would rather have you closer to the Maze. Just in case. Turk and I will catch up. Wait for me at the sign, but only for ten minutes, then continue."

Rigo headed for the road. Over the creak of saddle leather, I caught the clump of hooves as Izzie jogged to catch up with us. Rounding the Hump, the warhorses pointed their noses eastward and eased into a running walk. Our shadows stretched before us into distorted shapes with lumpy bodies and too many legs. Three miles away, the setting sun reflected off the taller buildings of Huerfano.

"Do you think Hester Lemprey is still in town?" Perry asked.

"Man, I hope not." The earlier concern crowded me in the saddle. Something bothered me about the Maze. About going inside. Maybe I was just freaked about Ol' Haggy MacHaggy running around in there.

Yeah. Maybe.

At the museum's sign, we paused and waited. Rigo kept one ear cocked back. Resting an edge of the shield on the saddle's fork, Perry slid her arm free and flexed it a few times, staring at the Maze.

"I wish I had a superpower," she said out of the blue. "Like for real."

I blinked. "What do you mean, a superpower?"

"You know. Something I could do that was totally mind-blowing. Like Izzie and Rigo are über-fast. You guys all have your maces. Even Hester Lemprey has that crystal wand. Me?" She smoothed a strand of Izzie's mane. "I've got nothing."

"You've got a killer softball pitch," Rigo offered. "That's kind of cool."

I cringed.

"Here comes Turk." Izzie swung her head around, ears pricked. "He looks like he's moving well. Javier must've gotten that shoe fixed."

"It's time we all had new ones…" The rest of Rigo's words faded like the setting sun. His body tightened. Neck raised, he stared toward town. "Izzie? Is that who I think it is?"

The sorrel pricked her ears. "Hester Lemprey." She snorted out the name in disgust. "Still a ways off, but approaching fast."

Dread seized me. I tightened my fingers around the mace's haft. "How far?" I squinted along the road. Was that a faint dust cloud?

"We need to go," Rigo said. "*Now*." He fidgeted from leg to leg, slashing his hindquarters—and my legs—with his tail. Even protected by denim, the wiry hairs stung my skin.

"What about Javier?" Perry struggled to get her arm through the grips while Izzie jigged beneath her.

Do I go with Perry and get her inside the Maze?

"Should we wait for him?" she asked.

But what about Dad? He'll try to take on the witch by himself to give us time. He'll need help. Heck, even the shield would be—

"Matt?" Perry leaned closer and poked me.

I knocked her hand away. "Sheesh, give me a second, will you?" My brain was a Slurpee drink, all thick and slow moving, as I tried to think. It didn't help that the sun ducked behind the mountains and left the dusk to take over. I licked my lips, mouth dry. "Okay, Izzie, you and Perry get inside the Maze, but stay by the Gate."

"No!" The sorrel flared her nostrils. "No way am I leaving—"

"And let me have that." I practically ripped the shield off Perry's arm. "Now, get out of here."

Rigo stretched out his neck and nipped the mare on the hindquarters. Izzie squealed, kicking out a back leg.

"Izzie, Matt's right this time," Perry shouted. "We're not helping. Just go already!" Still complaining, the sorrel whirled around and took off.

"Ready?" Rigo danced under me.

"Working on it." I fumbled with the shield, trying to shove my arm through the handles. The mace hanging from my wrist didn't help, nor did Rigo's salsa moves. Curling my fingers around the grip, I felt its weight; heavy, but not as bad as I had thought it'd be. With a flick of my wrist, I caught the mace's haft in my right hand. Leaving the reins loose on the stallion's neck, I tightened my knees and leaned forward.

"Go, Rigo!"

21

Rigo exploded. Even with my legs locked around his barrel, my rump hit the cantle as he went from a standstill to warp speed in three strides. Tearing along, his hooves barely touched the ground. His flying mane stung my face as the wind whined in my ears and pulled tears from my eyes, blurring my vision. I blinked them away.

Turk sprinted toward us, head thrust forward and legs chewing up the earth and spitting it out behind him. Dad rode low over the black's neck in a jockey's crouch, mace in hand and hat pulled tight.

"Keep going!" I hollered when they got within shouting distance. "Don't slow down!" Dad nodded once. We both knew it was harder for the black stallion to ramp back up to full speed carrying an adult rider.

As they thundered past in a cloud of dust, I braced my feet in the stirrups and grabbed the horn. "Now, Rigo!"

The stallion dropped his hindquarters, locked his back legs and slid along the road. Pivoting to the right, he wheeled around a massive sage bush, leaning so far to the inside I swore I skimmed a boot through the dirt. Branches snagged at my sleeve and snapped and cracked beneath his hooves. The spicy aroma filled my nostrils.

Rigo bounded back on the road, lowered his head, and kicked after Turk. Chuffing hard, he gained on the black one stride at a time—first Turk's tail, then my father low in the saddle, until both horses raced side by side, their heads bobbing in counter-rhythm.

"Perry and Izzie?" Dad shouted.

"Maze," I yelled back. *I hope.* With Izzie, it was always fifty-fifty.

A pair of giant, glowing eyes appeared in the distance. Headlights. They flickered and blinked, disappearing, and then reappearing. Over the stallions' thunder, I caught the rumble of Hester Lemprey's motorcycle. Panic knotted my gut. Our war-brothers were fast. But no horse could outrun an internal combustion engine. Maybe in rough terrain, but not on a road.

"Matt." Dad held out his hand. "The shield."

Clinging with my legs and grateful I was on Dad's left side, I wiggled my arm free and angled it toward him, the handles facing out. *Please*, I prayed, *don't let me drop it.*

"Hold on until I have it." Standing in the stirrups, my father leaned over and slid his arm through the grips, then plucked the shield from my hands and settled back in the saddle.

Ahead of us, the museum's sign loomed. Slowing down just enough to make the turn, the stallions careened into each other, squeezing my foot and leg between their bodies. I gasped in pain.

"Stop crowding me," Turk snarled.

"Stay in your lane, then," Rigo snapped back.

Untangling from each other, they hit the straightaway and sped up. Ahead, the Gate grew larger. Eyes watering from the speed, I squinted, desperate to spot Izzie and Perry in the corridor's shadow.

A yellow blur shot past my left ear. KAA-RACK! The fireball struck the cliff face near the Gate. Stone shrapnel exploded into the air. Heart rammed against the roof of my mouth, I looked back.

Hester Lemprey drove hunched over the motorcycle's handlebars, her head bare. One huge hand gripped both the handle and her crystal. Careening over the rough road, the bike bounced and jerked from side to side, sending rocks and bits of crushed vegetation flying. Steering one-handed, she slowed and aimed at us again.

Another blast. It arched over our heads and struck the ground at the horses' feet. Rigo twisted sideways so hard my jaw snapped. Only twelve years of riding under El Cid's relentless tutelage kept me in the saddle. Thank goodness for muscle memory.

I leaned forward, making myself as small as I could while trying to keep the saddle horn from punching me in the stomach. Dad shouted something. Turk faded back, swinging in behind Rigo. Rear guard. Another fireball hit a nearby *chamisa* bush, sending bits of flaming branches into the air. I squeezed my eyes tight as burning cinders stung my face.

Cold blackness. I felt Rigo stumble to a halt, ribs laboring. Gasping, I opened my eyes.

Weak with relief, I slumped in the saddle. On either side, the corridor's walls soared above us. A few yards away, Dad and Turk waited just inside the Gate. The heavy breathing of the warhorses filled the narrow space. Under my calf, I felt Rigo's heart hammering like mad. It slowed even as I laid a hand on my war-brother's wet shoulder.

"I can't believe you just outran a motorcycle."

"I was highly motivated," he panted, "by those fireballs on my tail."

The rumble of the approaching motorcycle grew louder. Rigo and I froze. The sound swelled, shaking the ground. Tiny rocks skittered down and landed with puffs of dust. Headlights flashed along one wall and disappeared.

"Matt!"

I swiveled around in the saddle. Izzie trotted toward us. Perry rode balancing in the stirrups, one hand on the horn.

"You okay?" Perry and I shouted at each other over the echoing roar.

"Yeah." I forced a smile. "Thanks to Rigo and…"

The roaring ceased. A last few pebbles pittered down. Glancing past me in the silence, Perry's eyes widened. I whipped around.

Straddling the bike, Hester Lemprey sat there glaring at us. With a savage move, she booted the bike's kickstand down and swung a leg over, then marched toward us, her features twisted with rage and her weapon aimed right at me. In the crystal's glow, the sorceress's face was a sickly yellow.

"You little cheat!" she screamed. Spit flew from her lips. "That casket was *empty*!"

She snapped her arm. The crystal spat out a fireball. I held my breath as it shrieked towards us. Next to me, Perry gasped.

KAA-RACK! The fireball bounced off the Gate's invisible barrier and shot away. More pebbles skittered from the walls. Eyes blazing, she flicked her wrist again. In a burst of sparks, the fireball ricocheted back, just missing her motorcycle.

Turk snorted. "Might want to work on your aim, sweetheart. That last one almost took out your hog."

The sorceress lowered her weapon. Her blue eyes were ice-cold. She stared at us, mouth working, then tilted her head back. Her gaze traveled along the towers, then back down again.

"It is a waste of your time, Hester Lemprey," my father called. "The wards have never failed."

"Not yet." Sneering, she stomped up to the entrance, dug her feet into the dirt, and raised her weapon over her head in a two-handed grip. "Let's see how those wards deal with magic a little more up close and personal—"

BOOM!

A bolt of lightning speared the ground between the toes of her work boots. Hester Lemprey lurched backward, feet stumbling over rocks and bushes and arms flailing; her crystal spat tiny fireflies with each jerk. She landed on her rear with a thud. I swore I heard her teeth clack together. Good. I hoped she bit her tongue off.

Rigo chuffed. "Now, *that's* what I'm talking about."

Perry looked at me; her mouth was a perfect O. She blinked. "The… the *wards*?"

"I know. Cool, right?"

Panting, Hester Lemprey staggered to her feet. Dusting off her clothes, she eyed the Maze, her stare sweeping the length of the walls before returning to the Gate. And us.

"What is she up to?" Rigo muttered.

Then, Hester Lemprey grinned. In the dusk, her pale face and wild expression reminded me of a *Día de los Muertos* mask. I shivered. Still smirking, she turned and walked back to her motorcycle.

Izzie snorted. "That's it? She's giving up?"

"We should be so lucky," Dad said over his shoulder.

Rummaging through one of the bike's saddlebags, the sorceress yanked out a daypack and a folded space blanket. Dumping the pack on the ground, she shook out the space blanket, and spread it across a large rock, then took a seat and rested the crystal across her knees.

"Oh, crud." My earlier worry flared to full horror. I watched, heart sinking, as the sorceress dug through the pack and pull out a bottle of water. Twisting off the cap, she took a drink.

"Matt?" Perry poked my arm. "What's she doing? What's going on?"

I wanted to hit myself with my mace. Why hadn't I thought of this scenario earlier? Had my father? "She's blocking the Gate. As long as she's out *there*, we're trapped in *here*."

"You mean," Perry stood in the stirrups and craned her neck, "she's *laying siege*?"

With a quiet word to Turk, Dad turned and rode toward us. His brows were knitted in frustration. "I had hoped to avoid this particular situation." He settled his hat more firmly on his head and motioned behind us. "For now, let us move further into the Maze."

Perry and I fell in behind Turk, our knees bumping as Izzie and Rigo walked side by side. The corridor was back-of-the-closet dim. I gave up trying to see much.

"What's the plan?" Perry's question ran along the corridor and repeated itself. *Plan... plan... plan.*

"The horses need rest," Dad said. "As do we. We will find a safe place to camp for tonight."

"And tomorrow?" I asked.

Dad glanced back over a shoulder. In the shadows, I caught the gleam in his eyes. He smiled coldly. "Tomorrow, we break the siege."

22

Trusting Rigo's better eyesight, I kept mine locked on the opening ahead. Echoes raced each other back and forth along the corridor. I slipped my mace through my hand and caught it by its business end, then ran a thumb over each sigil for luck. Because, holy moly, were we going to need a big ol' truck load of *that*.

Stepping out of the passage and into the Maze, Turk halted and sniffed the air, ears pivoting back and forth. He gave a low "all clear" grunt, then scramble-slid down the incline. Rigo and Izzie followed. Reaching the valley floor, the horses broke into a jog and headed for the western wall about a mile away. I nodded to myself as the horses arranged themselves into a single-file formation. Smart. Izzie planted herself behind Turk and in front of Rigo—the safest position for Perry. Even smarter.

Skirting the remains of the scientists' abandoned camp, Turk stomped through creosote and sage bushes instead of going around them, sending up an aromatic dust cloud. Dad sneezed repeatedly, complaining under his breath. Between the thud of hooves, the snap and crack of brush, and something metallic rattling in one of my saddle bags, I wondered if that creature heard us. With all that noise, how could she not? Under me, Rigo swung his head from side to side, nostrils working overtime.

I tugged on his mane. "Anything?"

"Hard to tell. That creepy critter was really dried out— barely had a scent. I got enough of a whiff so that I'll know if I smell her again."

Twisting in the saddle, Perry braced a hand on Izzie' haunch. "What does she smell like?"

Rigo thought for a moment. "Wet leather. Pumpkin seeds—yeah, don't ask—and a trace of skinner. Might've been a few of those meat monsters trapped inside the casket with her."

I zipped my hoodie up against the cooling evening air. "There weren't any when I opened it."

"Well, maybe the hag ate them," Perry said. "No, seriously. She kept herself alive by feeding on skinner. I'm guessing they were all crammed in there pretty tight, so it would be simple enough to just reach over and take a bite. Of course, the skinners could've done the same to her. You said, Matt, that one of her arms looked chewed on with the bone showing and—"

"Perry Vandermer," Dad said loudly, interrupting her. "To borrow a phrase from Ben: you are one sick puppy."

She nodded. "It's a gift."

We rode the rest of the mile in silence. The western cliff wall rose above our heads thirty or more feet. At its base, enormous chunks of sandstone—loosened by the never-ending assault of water and ice and wind—lay scattered about. The creeping dusk muted the sandstone's reds and yellows. Off to one side, a slot canyon split the wall.

Izzie walked closer and sniffed at the one-horse wide opening. "I smell water." A breeze from the canyon lifted her mane; on her back, Perry shivered. Tail flicking, the sorrel sniffed again, upper lip curled. "Hmm…"

"*Sí*, there is a seep back in there. One of the few dependable sources of water in the Maze." Dad dismounted and tugged the shield off, then propped it against a nearby rock. Rotating his shoulder, he flexed his arm a few times, then reached up and unfastened Turk's pack. Maneuvering the bulging saddlebags carefully off the stallion's haunch, he dropped them with a thud next to the shield. "Matt, water the horses. Except." He smacked his forehead with an open palm. "I forgot to remind you to pack the collapsible bucket."

"Actually, you did." I swung down. "Twice." I untied Rigo's saddle bags, then pulled them off and dumped them on the ground. "It's in one of these."

"I'll help." Reaching back, Perry fumbled with her daypack tied behind the saddle. "Let me get my hoodie first and—"

Izzie screamed.

The hag leaped out of the slot canyon, white hair flying. A shapeless dress hung in rags from her bony shoulders. Mouth stretched wide, she hissed and clawed at Perry's leg, twiggy fingers tipped with talon-like nails. Izzie reared, dancing on her hind legs and squealing in rage. Her front hooves scythed the air.

Perry grabbed for the horn. She missed. With a cry, she tumbled from the saddle and hit the ground. Sprawled in the dirt, she lay gasping for air, eyes wide with shock.

The hag darted under the warhorse's flailing hooves and disappeared in a blur. The air seemed to shudder. A moment later, the creature re-appeared on Perry's far side, claws extended, their tips weeping black droplets.

"Get away from her!" I unglued my boots from the ground and bolted for her, mace raised in a two-handed grip. Despair choked me—I knew I was too slow. Too slow and too late.

"NO!" With a desperate shout, Dad threw himself between Perry and the monster's claws, mace swinging. The hag shrieked and ducked, then launched herself at my father. They crashed to the ground in a writhing knot. A ripping sound. A blur. Then, the creature vanished into the air.

I skidded to a stop next to my father. Grimacing, he staggered to his feet, covered in dust and right sleeve torn into strips. Blood welled up and began soaking the material. Behind him, Perry scrambled away on hands and knees, then lurched to her feet, chest heaving.

"Perry. The cliff face." Izzie shoved the girl with her nose, almost knocking her back down again. "Go, go!" Perry sprinted away. The sorrel bolted after her.

Good thinking, Iz. I nodded to myself, then re-focused on Dad. "Where'd it go?" My gaze swept the area. "Maybe you nailed it."

Panting, Dad shook his head. "I missed. And then it disappeared." Right arm dangling uselessly, he switched the weapon to his left. "Is Perry all right? Is she safe?"

I checked over my shoulder. A few yards away, Perry stood pressed against the cliff face, Izzie in front of her, shielding her rider with her body. Standing on tiptoe, Perry peered over the sorrel's back and gave me a thumbs-up.

"She's fine. Izzie's guarding her over by the cliff. That monster would have to eat its way through Izzie to get to her."

Crowding our backs, Turk nosed my father's injured arm. "Javier? How bad?"

Dad winced. "Compared to what?" He dragged the back of his hand across his brow, almost whacking himself with his mace. Lowering his arm, he swayed, then blinked and shook his head.

I reached for him. "Dad?" Shame tore into me, chewing steadily through my chest. *I should've reacted faster. Instead, I just stood there while that hag—*

A soft hiss.

I froze. Out of the corner of my eye, I spotted a blur of motion. The hag shivered into view. I spun and swung my mace one-handed. She vanished in a swirl of wild hair.

I ground my teeth. "Dang it!"

A moment later, she re-appeared a few feet away from Dad. Turk lunged for her, teeth snapping like castanets. Once again, she simply disappeared. The big cheat. A chitter of laughter floated on the empty air. Dad swayed again. Taking a deep breath, he let it out slowly.

I braced a hand on his back. "You okay?"

"A little dizzy." He took another breath. "I will be fine."

Eyes white-rimmed with fury, Rigo paced back and forth in front of us, slapping me in the face with his tail each time he changed directions. He eyed my father.

"Nice move, Turk," Rigo sneered. "Letting Javier get sliced and diced like that."

"That's because *your* little rat of a rider," Turk snarled, "stood in the way, sucking his thumb, instead of—"

"Enough already," I snapped. "Both of you." Anger and worry and fear churned inside of me. "We've got to figure out how to…" The rest of the thought died and crept away. At the edge of my vision, the air shuddered again. "Nobody move," I whispered. "She's right next to me."

The warhorses froze in mid-stride, Rigo with one hoof in the air. I held my breath, eyes locked on the spot, and hands locked around the mace's haft. *Wait for it, wait for it…*

The creature winked into view.

I whipped my mace around in a backhanded swing, putting everything I had into the blow.

CRUNCH! The iron ball nailed the hag in the center of her chest. She stood there, her mouth gaping wider and wider and stretching the skin back on her skull. Then, without a sound, she crumbled and pitched forward face-down in the dirt.

My pulse whomping in my ears and mace at the ready, I inched closer and stared down at the hag. Astonishment and disbelief swept over me. Had I really destroyed it? Nah, couldn't have been *that* easy. I counted to ten, then nudged her with my weapon. Nothing happened. I poked her again, harder. A few strands of hair waved at me, stirred by the breeze. Reminding my lungs to breath, I lowered my weapon with a sigh of relief.

"Matt!"

I whirled around at Perry's scream, shoulders hunched.

My father lay sprawled on his back in the dirt. One hand still held his mace.

23

"One minute, he was watching you." Perry knelt next to my father. "And then the next, he just fell backwards."

I squatted on his other side. "Dad?" No answer. I watched his chest rise and fall. "He's breathing. That's good. Breathing is good." My focus shifted to his blood-soaked sleeve. "Um..."

"First aid supplies." Perry scrambled to her feet. "Where?"

I shook my head, trying to rattle the information loose. "I don't know. One of Turk's saddlebags."

She darted away. I eased apart the torn material. Four bloody gouges ran along his arm from shoulder to elbow. I gulped, then touched his shoulder; the skin felt hot and dry. How could he have a fever already?

Turk lowered his head, nose hovering over my father's face. "Those scratches look pretty deep."

"Gee, ya think?" For a moment, I was tempted to punch him right between the nostrils. The next moment, shame punched me instead. I don't know why I was taking it on him—it wasn't Turk's fault my father was hurt.

It was mine.

Perry returned. She handed me a small first aid kit and a bottle of water. Holding them in my hands, I sat there, waiting for my brain to kick in. Nothing.

"Here." She took the kit out of my hand. "Let me do it." She flushed the wounds with water, emptying the bottle, then cleaned them with antibiotic wipes and spray. With my help, she bound sterile pads in place with a long roll of white gauze, securing it tightly. "There."

"Thanks, Perry." Lowering Dad's arm, I looked up at her. "Where did you learn all this first aid?"

"Mom taught me the basics when I started going with her on digs." She sat back on her heels, scrubbing her hands along her jeans. Frowning, she continued to study my father.

"What's wrong?" I stuffed the rest of the supplies back in the box.

"Well," she said, "those wounds aren't all *that* serious. I don't see why he's unconscious. He's not weird about the sight of blood, is he? You know. How some people pass out when they see it?"

"Not even close. He deals with injuries all the time." Apprehension knotted my stomach into half hitches.

"That hag." Rigo stepped closer. His breath warmed the back of my neck. "I bet she carried some kind of poison or venom or something—didn't you see the tips of her claws? We need help, Matt. Someone who knows about this stuff."

"Who is there to call?" Turk said. "Ben's gone. The Navarres are on a plane somewhere, and the Montoyas are a day away. And anyway, none of them can do Javier any good if they can't get past that *bruja*. No, we need to get him out of here."

Izzie snorted. "I seriously doubt Hester Lemprey would give us a pass. More likely, she'd take advantage of Javier being sidelined."

Something touched my knee. I flinched, then looked down. My father's hand had flopped against my leg. It twitched again. "Dad?"

His eyelids fluttered, then opened into slits. "S-skinner..."

"It wasn't a skinner, Dad. It was that hag."

He swallowed. "Skinner venom. When you got bit. Remember... the medicine?"

I thought back to earlier in the summer when a skinner had chomped on me during a hunt and the misery of that night.

Vomiting, shaking with fever, my body curled in a ball from cramps. Hands moving me when all I wanted to do was sleep. Ben's voice breaking as he spoke. My father forcing some nasty tasting stuff between my lips . . .

"Oh! That stuff you gave me—that was for skinner venom?" Hope welled up, then slunk away. "But it was the hag that attacked you, Dad. Remember? Not a skinner."

"Same kind of poison," Dad rasped. "Just more..." he caught his breath and grimaced, "more potent."

"Izzie and I will go," Perry said. "You guys distract Hester Lemprey. We'll make for your house and—"

"No way." I cut her off. "You're staying here with my dad. *I'll* figure out a way to slip out by myself on foot—"

Rigo snorted. "Over my dead body."

"All of you, shut up and listen," Turk said. "We need to get Javier out of here and back home before he gets worse. That medicine slows the venom, but even with it, he's going to get a lot sicker. Better in his bed than laying out here in the dirt and cold."

I blinked. "How do you know this?"

Turk sniffed. "El Cid told me. When you got bit."

I looked down at my father. His eyes had closed, and his breath was harsh. I wanted him to wake up and tell me what to do. At least tell me how to stop messing up. *You chose the wrong son, Dad.* I squeezed my eyes and scrubbed my face with both hands. When I lowered them, everyone was looking at me. Waiting.

Frustration swelled my chest until my ribs creaked.

Why do I *have to make the call?* I wanted to scream in their faces. *What if it's the wrong one? Again!* I balled my hands into fists.

Sometimes, my son, there is no right or wrong decision. Dad's words whispered in my memory. *There is only the best decision you can make at the time.*

Great. Just great.

"Turk's right. We need to get Dad out of here." I frowned, mind racing. "Perry, if I can get him mounted on Turk, do you think you and Izzie could get him home?"

She nodded. "But what about you?"

Picking up my mace, I pointed it at the shield. "Rigo and I will go for Hester Lemprey. Well, for her crystal. And, yeah, there are a million reasons why it's a terrible plan. So, if you've got a better one—*any* of you—I'd be totally up for it."

A long silence.

"Okay, then." I squeezed my father's hand. "Hey." I waited until an eyelid peeled open. "How're you doing?"

"Oh, I have felt worse," he said in a weak voice. "Right now, however, I do not remember when." A corner of his mouth twitched.

"C'mon." I scooted around to his uninjured side and worked a hand under his shoulders. "We're leaving."

"That... that *bruja...*"

I explained my plan. "It's the best I could come up with." Steeling myself, I waited for the parental pushback.

Dad blinked up at the sky. I could almost see the wagon wheels turning in his head as he pondered the good, bad, and the ugly parts of the strategy. Then, he held out his good arm. I took it, helping him sit up, then eased him to his feet. Perry hovered nearby, hands outstretched and ready to catch him.

Face tight with pain, he nodded toward the shield. "Hold it close to your body. Easier to absorb the blows. From what we saw earlier, you will only have three or four seconds between each fireball." He reached for Turk's saddle. "Take the fight to her. Your mace can destroy her crystal, but so can the shield. Use it as a weapon." He raised his foot and set it in the stirrup, then grasped the horn with one hand. I boosted him up and helped him swing his leg over.

Just seeing my father mounted, even hunched over Turk's neck, made me feel a little less freaked out. I knew that if he could stay in the saddle, Turk would get him home.

Collecting Dad's hat from where it had rolled away during the fight, Perry clambered up on Izzie, then passed it to him. "Don't worry, Matt. We'll take care of him."

Side by side, Izzie and Turk walked across the valley and up the slope; Perry kept one hand on Dad's good arm. Rigo and I followed.

A numbing weariness crept over me. I shoved it aside. Instead, I tightened my fingers around the shield's grip, then raised and lowered my arm a few times. It felt like an extension of my limb. And, this time, its solid weight was reassuring. *I bet this shield has seen some insane action. Maybe, with its help, I can keep that witch busy long enough for everyone to get out of here.*

Right. And maybe Rigo could learn to play the cello.

As we rode through the corridor, my heart pounded so hard, I marveled it didn't crack a rib. Ahead of me, Dad swayed in the saddle. Even so, he held his mace ready in his left hand.

We stopped a few yards from the Gate. The sky was denim blue and empty, except for one over-achiever star just above the horizon. No, not a star. A planet. Probably Venus. Maybe Jupiter. *And why, oh why, am I thinking about astronomy when we are all about to die?*

"Sheesh, get your head in the game," I muttered to myself as I peered out. Still seated on the same rock, the sorceress's hair a pale blur in the dusk.

Okay then. Game on.

Hampered by mace and shield, I threw a leg over the horn and slid from the saddle, almost tipping over when I hit the ground. Pretending it wasn't awkward in the least, I straightened and looked around at everyone.

"Turk. Izzie," I said in a low voice, "when you see an opening, take it." I turned to Rigo. "I need you to stay here, too." I clamped my hand over his nostrils to silence his protest. "No, listen. You're wicked fast, but those fireballs are faster. I can't focus if I'm worried about you getting barbequed." I let go of his nose.

My war-brother flattened his ears. "Barbeque or not, if things get too hot, I'm coming after you."

I tugged his forelock. "You better."

"Matt?" Perry reached down and squeezed my shoulder. "Watch out for flying monkeys, okay?"

I managed a smile, lips stiff, then glanced up at my father. He nodded once and said something too low for me to catch. Didn't matter. I think I knew what it was anyway.

My knees newborn foal-flimsy and my pulse roaring in my ears, I raised my weapons and marched through the Gate.

24

Hester Lemprey uncrossed her legs and stood. Her gaze drifted past me. "Where's the rest of the posse?"

"It's just me." Forcing my legs to keep moving, I angled away from the Gate. I swear she grew bigger with each step. And she was already plenty big enough.

"What? You drew the short straw?" She gestured at the shield. "By the way, that piece of cosplay isn't going to work."

"Sure it will." I struck the Del Toro moon with my mace—I figured Santiago wouldn't mind. The shield rang like church bells exalting Sunday Mass.

The sorceress sneered. "Looks like someone wants to run with the big dogs. Fine with me." Extending her arm, she aimed her weapon at my face. The crystal's glow welled up. "Fire in the hole," she cried, and snapped her wrist.

The fireball hurtled toward me. I braced myself, hunkering down behind the shield. KAA-RACK! The impact felt like a mule kick from Turk. Sparks flew into the air. I staggered back, arm and shoulder screaming from the blow.

One Mississippi. Two Mississippi. Three Mississippi. Four—

KAA-RACK! A second fireball struck the edge of the shield; it twisted to one side, wrenching my arm. Pain zinged along my wrist and up my elbow, my fingers going numb. Another bolt slammed into the shield; it jerked from my deadened grasp and clattered to the ground.

I lunged for it. A blast hit the spot where my boots had been a second before. The mace swung around by its strap and glanced off my skull. Stars burst across my vision. Eyes watering, I grabbed the shield in both hands, then rolled over onto my back, bringing it up just in time.

KAA-RACK!

I ordered at myself to move, move, move before she powered up again. Gasping for breath, I lurched to my feet, shield at chest level and mace dancing on its leather strap. My left wrist throbbed. Legs wobbling, I backed away. The sorceress stalked toward me, the crystal moon-yellow in the deepening dusk.

Another blast. The shield bucked in my hands. Its upper edge clipped me under the chin and snapped my head back; white-hot agony lanced through my tongue. Tears welled up, blinding me.

A moment later, rage exploded inside of me, shoving aside the pain. It swelled my chest until my ribs creaked. Blinking the tears away, I spat a bloody mess to one side. *Take the fight to her,* my father's voice whispered in my head. Gritting my teeth, I shoved my left arm through the grips, ordered my fingers to hold on, then caught my mace by its haft. I raised it over my head.

"SANTIAGO!"

Mouth sagging open, Hester Lemprey blinked in surprise. Guess she wasn't used to folks going on the offensive and getting in her face.

I charged, legs churning and head lowered, and barreled into her, my shield a battering ram. It was like getting punched in the chest by a giant fist. Breathless, I bounced backwards, mace arm flailing and feet tripping over rocks. One heel caught a snag. I toppled and hit the ground. The shield landed on top of me. Lungs struggling for air, I screamed at my arms and legs to move, get up, do *something*. My body told me no, it was fine where it was, and thanks anyway. I rolled my head to one side.

I wasn't the only one knocked flat by the collision. Hester Lemprey was staggering to her feet. A bloody line curved like a crescent from her temple to the corner of her mouth. She touched the cut, then looked at her fingertips. "You little punk. That's going to leave a scar."

Legs finally working again, I pushed the shield aside, then rolled to my elbows and knees and clambered to my feet. My entire body ached; each cut and bruise throbbed in rhythm with my thundering heart. I squeezed my hand around my mace.

Movement behind the witch. I looked past her to the Gate. My heart stopped, then started up again with a painful thud.

Rigo burst out of the Gate, nostrils stretched wide and eyes white-rimmed with wrath. Kicking up dirt behind, he hit top speed in three strides as he hurtled toward the sorceress. Hester Lemprey whirled around. A pause. Then, with a flick of her wrist, she fired at my war-brother.

I screamed.

Jackrabbit-nimble, Rigo twisted in mid-stride. His head snapped to one side. He faltered, shook his mane, then leaped back into the fray.

"Rigo," I cried. "Get out of here!"

Wild-eyed, the sorceress backed up a step and pointed her wand. The crystal's glow swelled, its sickly yellow light growing stronger. She thumped her chest with her free hand. "Come at me," she shouted, weapon raised.

Rigo sped up. His black mane and tail streamed behind him, war banners accompanied by drumming hoof beats. My breath caught at the sight. In spite of everything, goose bumps ran up my arms. Because I knew exactly what was going to happen.

Eleven hundred pounds of Andalusian war stallion plowed into her.

Hester Lemprey's feet left the ground. She flew backwards, arms and legs flapping. Her wand spun away and disappeared. Landing on her back with a thud I felt through the soles of my boots, she skidded along, leaving a furrow in the dirt. Coming to a stop, she lay sprawled on the ground, mouth opening and closing like a trout on a riverbank.

Heck, yeah, I laughed.

Picking up the shield, I pulled it back on my arm, then limped toward her, Rigo at my shoulder, his ribs heaving and teeth bared. Blood oozed from the tip of his ear. We stopped a few yards away, wary.

Hester Lemprey groaned. She sat up, wheezing, then staggered to her feet, one eye on me and Rigo. Dust coated her face and jacket and crusted the cut on her cheek; dried vegetation stuck to her hair. Backing away, she scanned the area.

As if Rigo wasn't enough, Perry darted out of the Maze. Before I could yell at her, she sprinted a few yards, hurdling over bushes and rocks, then skidded to a halt and snatched something from the ground. She bolted back inside the Gate to Turk's side. What the heck was she doing?

"Hey, Hester. Look what I got." Perry waved the sorceress's crystal over her head. "Finders, keepers, right?"

"Don't be so proud of yourself, Hermione." Hester Lemprey pressed a hand to her ribs. "Its power won't work for you."

"What a coincidence." Perry grinned. "Because in a few moments, its power won't work for you, either."

She said something to my father, who nodded and straightened in the saddle. Shuffling back a step, Perry held the crystal up in the air like an Olympic torchbearer and turned her face away, shielding it with her free arm.

My father's awkward left-handed swing had about as much force as a sparrow's wing. Even so, it was enough. The crystal shattered like a dropped light bulb and showered Perry in a cloud of shimmering dust. She fanned it away.

"*NOOO,*" Hester Lemprey shrieked.

"Yes!" I punched my mace into the air, almost clipping Rigo on the chin.

Hester Lemprey stared at Perry. All color drained from her face. She started to speak, then closed her eyes and slumped down on a rock. Bowing forward with a moan, she buried her face in her hands.

Afraid to lower the shield or my mace, I waited, even though my arms were begging for a time out. Eyes still on Hester Lemprey, I spoke to Rigo out of the corner of my mouth. "Now what do we do?"

"Let's start with killing her," he muttered back, "and then go from there."

I shifted from foot to foot, stomach churning at the notion. Because this wasn't some scene from a movie or TV show. This was real life. And in real life, a kid doesn't walk up to a person and club them to death. *Not* this *kid, anyway.*

Funny what a guy learns about himself on the battlefield.

Hester Lemprey lifted her head and stared at me. "Before you kill me," she said in a flat tone, "tell me one thing—why'd you lock up an empty coffer?"

Wow. I was expecting a lot of things. That question wasn't one of them. "W-what?"

With a weary sigh, she waved a hand around. "Look, you won. So why not just answer my question. There wasn't anything inside the Red Casket, so why seal it? Was it part of the scam?"

"Actually, the seal kept—" Rigo began.

I elbowed him. Hard. "No, you first. Why did *you* want the casket so badly? What did you think was inside of it?"

Her jaw worked, like she was chewing on something nasty. After a long moment, she shrugged. "Okay, fine. I'll play. Got nothing to lose." She sniffed, then swiped her nose with the back of a hand. "The question isn't *what* was inside, but *who*."

I rolled my eyes. "Okay. *Who?*"

"My sister." Her faint smile lasted about a nano-second. If that long.

The ground rocked beneath me. I wavered, forgetting how to breath. "Your... your *sister?*" I recalled the gouges on the inside of the lid. Had Hester's sister tried to claw her way out?

"Yeah, my sister. She disappeared years ago. We never knew what happened to her. I had promised our parents before they died that I'd find out. I recently heard rumors that one of you Knights—don't know from which family—had imprisoned her in a coffer for no reason."

"There had to be a reason," I said weakly. "She must've done *something.*" Out of the corner of one eye, I spied Dad and Perry riding toward us.

Hester Lemprey twitched a shoulder. "Okay, maybe there was. She *is* one heck of a caster—our family is famous for our spell casting. And, yeah, she has a temper. *Had* a temper." The sorceress looked away. "Anyway, I thought if anyone had a chance of staying alive inside that thing, she would. She's got some serious magical abilities." She sighed. "I guess the rumor was wrong."

Scrubbing a hand through her short hair, she dislodged bits of vegetation. She flicked them away as the rest of my family joined us. The top of Perry's head glittered—like she had run amok in a craft store. Not a good look.

"What happened to you?" Hester Lemprey nodded at my father's bandaged arm.

Jaw clenched, Dad pushed himself upright. "I fell off my horse."

"*You* fell off a horse. Yeah, right." She eyed his torn sleeve and the blood-dotted gauze. "Looks more like something went after you with teeth or claws..." Her voice trailed off.

Uh-oh. My mouth dried up. What if she had another weapon? Maybe a spell or something worse. Never trust a witch, right?

Eyes narrowed with suspicion, Hester Lemprey slowly rose to her feet, gaze shifting from me to Dad to the Maze and back again. "There are very few things in this world that can take a Knight out of the game," she said slowly. "And since word on the street is that you guys have those skinners locked tight, I'm guessing something *else* got to you."

Perry and I peeked at each other. I tried to keep my face blank. Yeah, epic failure there.

"I *knew* it." Hester Lemprey's eyes blazed at our expressions. "My sister *was* trapped inside the Red Casket after all. Where is she now? Still in the Maze?"

I swallowed a lump of foreboding. What did it matter if she found out her sister was actually dead? Nothing she could do about it.

"And, wow," the sorceress gloated, "look at her going head to head with the famous Javier Del Toro, even after being trapped for so long. I'm surprised she had the strength; that would be my sister, all right." Beaming, she hopped up on the rock and craned her neck. "Gretel?" she hollered. "Hey, Gretel. It's me. Hester. I'm out here."

Izzie flattened her ears. "The hag's name was *Gretel*?"

"That fits." Turk said. "Because she's dead as an oven door now." He clopped his lips in amusement.

"Turk," I hissed. "*Shut. Up.*"

Too late.

Hester Lemprey stiffened. "What was that? About my sister?"

"Nothing." Perry, Izzie, Rigo, and I all said at the same time.

Turk snorted. "What's the big deal, guys? The Valkyrie here got her wings clipped. All she's packing now is attitude and a smart mouth. Who gives a rip if she knows or not. So, yeah, Brunhilda, your sister *was* in the Red Casket—talk about a strong family resemblance. She went after Perry, then attacked Javier, then tried for the rest of us. Matt here took her out with his mace. She's deader than dead." The black stallion curled his lip. "How do *you* like running with us big dogs?"

25

Face moon-pale, Hester Lemprey stared at Turk. Rage and something else twisted her features. Then, her focus swung to me. Still standing on the rock, she towered over me, her glare Arctic blue and just as cold.

Goose bumps snapped to attention on my arms and neck. I wanted to crawl behind Rigo, or even better, Turk.

"All these years," the sorceress said softly, "of not knowing where she was or if she was even still alive. Keeping the faith and keeping the search going when everyone urged me to give it up and move on. And now you're telling me I lost my sister again? This time for good?"

Tongue glued to the roof of my mouth with fear, I squeezed the haft until my fingers cramped and waited for the explosion. Rigo crowded closer to me, his hide twitching. Guess he felt the chill, too. A rumble rose in his chest.

She sneered. "Down, Fido. I'm unarmed, remember?"

Hester Lemprey continued to stare at me, eyes half-lidded and head cocked, like she was memorizing my face.

Creepy, followed by a big ol' helping of creepier. I wished she'd just attack us and get it over with.

Except Perry couldn't help me and Dad wasn't in any shape to do battle. Which meant it was all up to me and the warhorses, and even with their help, I didn't know how much fight *I* had left. My chin throbbed. A wide scrape along my back stung every time my shirt rubbed against it. Both elbows felt like someone had take sandpaper to them. Even my tongue ached.

Without a word, she jumped down from the rock, her boots crushing an innocent sage bush. I tensed and lifted both shield and mace back up with a grunt. Ears pinned flat and nostrils flared, Rigo stomped a hoof in warning.

Hester Lemprey smiled. "Feeling a little panicky, are we? Worried about what I'm going to do? What's going to happen next? Who else might get hurt?" Her grin vanished as quickly as it appeared. "Well, get used to that feeling." She backed toward her motorcycle. Reaching it, she threw a leg over and kicked it to life. The engine's roar shook the ground.

"End her, Matt," Rigo said in a low voice. "Before she gets away."

"I-I can't." *I don't want to. I don't think I even can.* Because what if Dad had been right and she still had some humanity left?

"Remember what I said about being really good at payback? I wasn't bragging." She raised her chin. "You know, I would've been happy to just free my sister and leave you guys alone. Gretel was the one who was obsessed with settling the score against you Knights, not me. I was always more in the 'an eye for an eye just leaves everyone half blind' camp."

It isn't my fault, I wanted to scream. *I didn't know about your sister or why you wanted the Casket. I was just trying to keep my family safe.*

"But now? Now, I think I'm going to go with revenge. Just as you destroyed the two most important things in my life, I'm going to return the favor—ten-fold. And here's the best part." Her smile reappeared. Its manic creepiness would've made a jack-o'-lantern proud. "You'll never know when I'm going to strike. Your family, horses, friends—even your barn and house—will always be at risk. I'm going to take them from you, one by one, until you're left with nothing, Matt Del Toro."

Rigo and I started toward her at the same time.

She revved the engine and wheeled around, punishing the bike's tires. With a spray of pebbles and sand and exhaust, she roared away. On trembling legs, I watched the red taillights getting smaller and smaller until they winked out in the night.

I knew I should've been flattened to the ground by what just happened—*and is going to happen*—but all I felt was a bone-snapping fatigue. A warm droplet splashed on my neck. I touched it, then studied my fingers. Blood. I looked up at Rigo. "Did you know the tip of your left ear is missing?"

"Yeah, she nicked me with one of those fireballs." He rolled an eye, trying to see. "Does it look weird?"

"Well." I stood on tiptoe. "There's a definite notch. I'll take care of it when we get back."

I sighed. My exhaustion grew, almost buckling my knees. Dizzy, I leaned against my war-brother for a moment, then pushed away; I had an injured father to get home and patched up. I stepped over to Izzie and hoisted the shield to Perry. "Take this. I'll ride with Dad."

We headed home at a slow walk, Perry and Izzie in the lead. My father rode slumped in his seat, chin on his chest and eyes at half-mast. I could tell it was all he could do to stay in the saddle. By the time we reached the Hump, the rest of the stars had shown up for their nightly exhibition.

Rounding the hill, I would've cheered if I had any energy. *Now all I have to worry about is seeing to Dad and fixing the biggest roast beef sandwich—*

"Hey, Matt?" Perry spoke over her shoulder. "Not to freak you out, but I think someone's in your house. The lights are on."

My heart *ka-thudded.* The porch light was on, all right. I thought I spotted the living room lamps as well.

"It could be Ben." Izzie slowed, waiting for the rest of us to catch up.

"Maybe, but I doubt it." My cell phone chimed. I leaned to one side and pulled it out of my back pocket. The Navarre sigil—linked chains crisscrossing each other to form an eight-point starburst—filled the screen. *I wish Roman and Kathleen were here right now instead of on a plane. I sure could use their help.*

I tapped the device. "Hi, Roman. Man, am I glad you called. Dad's hurt and Ben's gone." *And because of me, there's a sorceress out there that wants to kill us.*

"Easy, *chico*. Where are you now?" Beyond Roman's voice, I heard Kathleen asking something, then the bang of drawers opening and closing.

"Riding up the drive. We're all okay. Well, except for Dad." I glanced at my father. His eyes were closed, and his head nodded in rhythm with Turk's stride. Turning away, I whispered into the phone. "I don't know what to do for him. I think there's some medicine—"

The front door opened. Light leaped across the yard. A huge figure followed, taking the steps in one giant stride.

Roman Navarre—the lighter half of the heavy cavalry.

My throat tightened at the sight of the bull-necked Knight, shoulder-length hair pulled back in its customary ponytail, hurrying toward us. Reaching Turk's side, Roman laid a broad hand on my father's knee and peered up at him.

"We leave the country for the first time in years," Roman said, "and you, my friend, decide to take on a *bruja* single-handedly."

"Oh, no, not I." Dad smiled weakly at me, then pushed his hat back with an unsteady hand. "And what are *you* doing here? I thought you and Kathleen were still—"

"Stop talking and dismount before you fall out of the saddle and embarrass Turk. Here. Give me that." He plucked Dad's mace from his grasp and slipped the leather strap around his own meaty wrist.

"Good to see you, Roman." Turk huffed a long breath. "How did you know we needed some backup?"

"Ben called me and told me everything." Roman offered a hand to Dad. "We will talk more once I get Javier inside." The large hunter eased my father from the saddle, then half-escorted, half-carried him into the house.

"Go with them, Matt." Perry said. "I'll take care of the horses." She shooed me away.

Wincing, I swung my leg over and dismounted, holding onto the stirrup strap until my head stopped swimming. Various bruises and cuts reminded me they needed some attention, too. I limped across the yard and up the porch; each step felt like my boots were full of concrete. I dragged my sorry self through the front door.

Kathleen O'Riley Navarre stood at the kitchen counter, digging through our first aid drawer. In the overhead light, her hair, a perfect match to Izzie's coat, stuck out in a fiery halo around her head. She paused, blue eyes tight with worry, as I sank down at the table.

"Why, you look like Rigo dragged you facedown through the dirt." Kathleen went back to her rummaging. "For a couple o' miles, I might add." She pulled out a small, flattish bottle made of dark brown glass—I swore it looked like an old vanilla bottle—and held it up to the light, tilting it back and forth. "This should be enough for our fine man."

"How's Dad?"

"I'm on my way to him right now. But first." She joined me at the table. Scooting her chair closer, she studied my face, eyeing the cuts and bruises, then the rest of me. "Anything critical?"

"Nothing I can't handle with ice and stuff."

"Tough boyo, eh?" I noticed her Irish accent, usually as faded as prairie grass after a dry summer, had greened up. She peered past me. "Where's Perry?"

"Taking care of the horses. Oh, and Rigo lost the tip of an ear."

"Right." Kathleen rose, bottle in one hand. "Once I get Javier settled, I'll patch up whoever else needs patching. And Matt?"

"Yeah?"

"There's an auld saying amongst my people: 'There is nothing so bad that it couldn't be worse.'" She squeezed my shoulder and left.

I couldn't sleep. There were hornets buzzing around inside of me; each one was a flashback of the last few days, and every replay was a needle prick of their stingers. Sick of lying in the dark with my guilt and staring up at the living room ceiling, I made a face, then rolled off the sofa, naturally stubbing my toe on the coffee table leg. I winced, stifling a cry.

I had given up my room to Roman and Kathleen since they were spending the night. Ben had caught them while they were changing planes in Denver.

"We skipped the final leg to Albuquerque, rented a car instead, and drove down here as quickly as we could," Kathleen had said. "Ben took quite the risk letting us know what was happening, both here and at our ranch. Brave lad."

"Our daughter," Roman had explained to Perry. "She has my good looks and her mother's fierce independence. Ben is lucky Jo did not use her mace on him."

Smiling at the memory, I started for the kitchen, then changed my mind and padded down the hall, past Perry's closed door, then the Navarres'.

Dad's door stood ajar. Easing it wider, I poked my head inside. A night light—the Batman one I used as a kid—bathed the room in a soft glow. Wearing a worn but clean T-shirt, my father was leaning against the headboard, eyes closed and bandaged arm resting on a spare pillow.

"If that is Roman," he murmured, "please find my mace and put me out of my misery."

I shuffled over and took a cautious seat on the edge of the mattress. "Not doing so good?"

"Why, between the fever and the bouts of vomiting," he said, "I am having the time of my life." He opened his eyes. "How are *you* feeling?"

"Like I got caught on foot in a stampede." I poked a finger through a hole in the knee of my pajama pants and sighed. *You'll never know when I'm going to strike. Your family, horses, friends—even your barn and house—will always be at risk. I'm going to take them from you, one by one, until you're left with nothing, Matt Del Toro.* I gritted my teeth, trying to squeeze her voice out of my head. Guilt was a semi-truck parked on the back of my neck.

Dad stopped my finger from doing more damage to my pjs. "You are thinking of what she said, no?" He kept hold of my hand.

I nodded, unable to meet his eyes. "She's going to kill us, isn't she?" *Please say no. Please say you know how to fix this. That you have a plan.*

"Oh, no doubt Hester Lemprey will try. But she will fail."

His matter-of-fact tone yanked my head up. "H-how do you know?"

"I am your father. I know everything."

"Yeah, right." A grin tugged at a corner of my mouth. I let it loose for a moment.

"And I know that my son needs to hear that his papá is so very proud of him." His fingers tightened around mine. "You fought and defeated a sorceress armed with only a mace and shield, no training, and vast courage."

"But... but... I screwed up by selling the casket to her in the first place." My throat tightened. Pushing past the wad o' misery, I swallowed hard and blurted out the truth. "If it wasn't for me, none of this would've happened."

"Ah, *mijo*. You carry too much of the responsibility for all this. Do you not realize that in the end, Hester Lemprey would have eventually killed us to obtain the casket? You simply forced her hand earlier."

I shook my head. "But that was just *luck*. I mean, I didn't *plan* it. It just happened."

Dad shrugged, then winced. "In the end, what does it matter? Luck happens—something you will come to appreciate as a leader. And speaking of *that*, I must apologize to you."

My jaw sagged. "F-for *what*?"

"This guilt you carry—it is my fault. No, listen, *por favor*. I should have made certain you understood that the leadership of our family and its mission is many, many years in the future. I plan on being around for those years.

All *you* need to do now, my son, is grow up and grow strong and learn from me and the warhorses. Your day will come," his mouth twitched, "but it is not this day."

I blinked. Did he just quote *The Lord of the Rings*?

"We will talk more tomorrow. For now, get some sleep. And Matt?" His gaze sharpened, a hawk on the hunt. "Evil things have sought to end the Knights and their families for centuries. Yet here we are. Trust that your papá has a few tricks of his own." He stared past me at the window's black glass and sighed. "And it may be time to make a long overdue phone call," he said in a low tone, as if speaking to himself. Before I could ask what he meant, he waved me away with a gentle smile, then closed his eyes.

I tiptoed out of the room. Shielding my father's words in my heart like a candle flame, I headed back to the living room, my body and soul lighter. The burden I'd been hauling around for the last three days was gone. Or at least didn't weight as much. Sure, in the future, I'd need to shoulder that load again, when I took over from Dad, but not now. Not yet.

I eyed the sofa and the rumpled bedding, then bent down and found my shoes. Tugging them and my hoodie on, I tiptoed out of the front door, easing the screen door closed with a heel.

Skirting the barn, I rounded the far corner and paused. The practice field stretched out before me, enjoying the stars. At its far edge, El Cid's marker was a tiny smudge of white.

A feeling like homesickness blew through me.

Right then, I'd have given almost anything to have the gray stallion standing next to me, his coat warm and silky under my palm, and his deep voice rambling on as he reassured me it'd be okay. That he and my father had a clever plan or an archaic spell or a little-known use of our maces. That he, too, was proud of me. And that he loved me and always would. No matter what I did.

A large shape stepped out of the building's shadow.

My heart slammed into the roof of my mouth. I jumped, almost tripping over my own feet. The shape chuffed softly and ambled closer.

Stupid Rigo. In the dark, the white bandage on the tip of his ear seemed to hover in midair over his head.

"Not. Cool." I patted my chest, coaxing my heart back to normal speed. "What are you doing out here?"

"I'm a horse. This is a field. What do you think I was doing?" He flicked his uninjured ear toward the house. "How's Javier?"

"Not great, but better. Knowing him, he'll be out of bed tomorrow, arguing with Kathleen that he's well enough to go for a light jog. Probably to Nebraska and back."

"He's a tough *hombre*, that's for sure." Rigo nudged me in the chest with his nose. "So are you."

Kicking at a clod of dirt and grass, I blew a raspberry. "Not even close."

"Are you kidding? Matt, you took on a wicked witch and her wand. With only a shield and a mace. That's tough in *my* stall."

Maybe he was blowing smoke, but it still felt all kinds of good to hear a version of my father's sentiment from my war-brother. The growing certainty—fueled by my conversation with Dad—flared in my chest: Sorceress or not,

Hester Lemprey was going to have to bring her A game if she thought she could defeat us Del Toros.

"You did okay yourself," I said. "We would've never destroyed her crystal if it hadn't been for you charging her. That was some hit. And it saved my life. She would've killed me if you hadn't made your play when you did."

"Javier said take the fight to her, so I did. Not my finest move, but it got the job done. And I shouldn't have let you face her alone. I'll never make that mistake again." He pointed his nose up at the stars, checked the night breeze, then lowered it. "Roman was right."

"*Roman*? About *what*?"

"He told me, when I volunteered to help you guys after El Cid died, that hunting with Javier would be a solid learning opportunity. That's one of the main reasons I originally came north, you know. Get a chance to see the legend in action and all that."

"Guess that's why you decided to stay and join Team Del Toro, huh?" I straightened his forelock.

"Actually, it wasn't. I mean, sure, I'm learning a lot from Javier. And even from Turk, but don't tell him I said that." He chuffed. "No, your dad was the reason I *came*, but he wasn't why I *stayed*."

"Then why?" The old question crept out of the shadow.

"C'mon, Matt. You know why."

Even as I shook my head, I realized I no longer cared. I was just grateful he had.

He lowered his neck and pressed his forehead against mine and let out a soft breath. The home-sweet-home aroma of horse and grass wafted over me. I closed my eyes and pressed back.

"I stayed, Matt," he said after a moment, "because you asked me to.

Author's Note

Dear Fellow Reader,

Writing the next book in a series is both a joy and a challenge. Joy, because returning to the Del Toro ranch and hanging out with Matt and Perry and the warhorses is the Best Thing Ever. Challenge, because so much of the world building had already been established in *Del Toro Moon*, and I had to write to what is called "canon." In other words, I had to follow the rules set down in the first book.

Rules are not necessarily a bad thing when it comes to art, be it literature, visual arts, music, or the performing arts. Our brains are incredibly creative, even when we have to color inside the lines. Within those lines, however, our imagination is boundless. For example, I needed a weapon that could stand up to Hester Lemprey's fireballs. When Javier tried to use his mace, it just didn't work. So, I read through *Del Toro Moon* and realized the weapon I needed was already right there, hanging over the fireplace in their living room.

These are the serendipitous moments in writing I never see coming, but I'm always surprised and grateful when they show up. Although, when it comes to art, I do not believe in happy accidents. I believe parts of our brains are relentlessly working away, creating stuff behind our backs; we just don't realize it at the time. The trick to good art is to recognize the good stuff when it arrives.

I hope you'll saddle up and ride along with me on Matt's future adventures. Remember to wear sunscreen. See you on the trail.

Head on over to the official website and explore the world of *Del Toro Moon*. The site is loaded with activities, videos, maps, information about the author, as well as projects for kids and teachers and parents. Join the posse at www.deltoromoon.com.

Del Toro Moon (Book One in the *Del Toro Moon* series):
    2019 Colorado Book Award Winner for Juvenile
        Literature
    2018 Reading the West Longlist Pick
    2018 Moonbeam Children's Book Silver Award for
        Juvenile Fantasy

Acknowledgements

Since my husband is first in my heart, he gets to be first on this list, too. Thanks, Wes, for being the Swiss army knife of my life.

I wish to thank Emma Nelson and the incredible folks at Owl Hollow Press for working their hindquarters off for me and my books. When Emma proposed turning *Del Toro Moon* into a series, I couldn't saddle up fast enough. Working with her is a straight up joy. Emma, you have a rare combination of vision, passion, and enthusiasm—and a wicked sense of humor; I have yet to get through a Skype visit with you without laughing so hard I cry. I'm beyond grateful and proud to be part of the OHP parliament.

Once again, editor extraordinaire Olivia Swenson worked her magic. The resulting version of *The Red Casket* exceeded all my expectations, thanks to her keen eye for both trees and forests. In so many ways, we wrote this book together. A good editor will ride into the Maze with you. An outstanding editor will show you the way back out. Olivia, if I ever sell medieval chests on the black market, I am totally splitting the money with you.

Caroline Geslison (publicity manager) and Hannah Smith (acquisitions) are the finest *compradres* anyone could wish for. One day, my friends, we will take that ride together in real life.

Milorad Savanović (cover artist) blew my mind. He created the hands down, straight up most perfect cover for this book. Thank you, Milorad, for your talent and patience and enthusiasm.

Like Perry, I think collective nouns are one of the coolest things about the English language. I tried and tried to think of a clever one for a group of sorceresses, but it was my sister, Kelly Austin, who came up with "a secret of sorceresses." Thanks, Kelly, for being the best sister in the whole dang world. And thank you to my brothers, Derek and Lee, for being so supportive of all my books. You two are my favorite brothers, you know.

And now I get to thank the most important person of all: YOU. It is because of readers like you who told their friends and families about *Del Toro Moon* that this second book is in your hands. Even better, there are more Wild West adventures a-coming for the Del Toros and their friends. I'd love to hear from you and I answer every single email, so stop by and visit me at www.darbykarchut.com.

About the Author

Darby Karchut is a multi-award-winning author, dreamer, and compulsive dawn greeter. A proud native of New Mexico, she now lives in the foothills of the Rocky Mountains, where she runs in blizzards and bikes in lightning storms. When not dodging death by Colorado, Darby is busy wrangling words.

Her books include the best-selling middle grade novels *Del Toro Moon* and *Finn Finnegan*. Visit the author at www.darbykarchut.com

Made in the USA
Coppell, TX
16 January 2020